Tom Kelly

Time and Chance

A novel. Part 3

Tom Kelly

Time and Chance
A novel. Part 3

ISBN/EAN: 9783337052409

Printed in Europe, USA, Canada, Australia, Japan

Cover: Foto ©Andreas Hilbeck / pixelio.de

More available books at **www.hansebooks.com**

TIME AND CHANCE

A Novel

BY

MRS. TOM KELLY.

"Fate, Time, Occasion, Chance, and Change. To these
All things are subject but eternal Love."

IN THREE VOLUMES.

VOL. III.

LONDON:
HURST AND BLACKETT, PUBLISHERS,
13, GREAT MARLBOROUGH STREET.
1882.

CONTENTS

OF

THE THIRD VOLUME.

BOOK III.—LOVE AND ART.

BOOK III.

LOVE AND ART.

" . . . Se tu segui tua stella
Non puoi fallire a glorioso porto."

DANTE.

". . . If thou thy star do follow
Thou canst not fail thee of a glorious port."

TRANSLATION BY LONGFELLOW.

VOL. III.   B

TIME AND CHANCE.

CHAPTER I.

THE END OF A SWEET SPRING SONG.

" Ah, why art thou sad, my heart ?   Why
    Darksome and lonely ?
Frowns the face of the happy sky
    Over thee only? . . . . . .
As a bird, though the sky be clear,
    Feels the storm lower :
My soul bodes the tempest near
    In the sunny hour."
                 BULWER LYTTON.

THE spring songs had begun again, and
myriad voices were swelling the

annual chorus in the woods of Kerinveau.
The innumerable waters were making
jocund music, and the white gulls were
winging their happy ways over the loch;
and all was fair on the hills, bright in the
valleys, and calm on the sea. The salmon
were leaping the falls going up stream,
and enjoying their adventurous experiences, some of them shunning the shallows
where cunning flies floated, merciless
and cruel; while others, keen to see and
very avaricious, despite the warnings of
their elders, darted to the surface, but
as quickly dived back to the deep pools,
ere temptation became too strong.

Every creature was glad because winter
had gone; the mysterious feeling of spring

had got into the nerves of all living things; some seemed intoxicated by it and laughed outright, or merrily carrolled from dawn till eve. The frequent scamper of the deer in the lonely glens at the head of the loch was less timorous now that the breathing, scathless time had come, and the sentinels were at peace, and could roam as they pleased. The shaggy cattle, with their serious, untidy faces, appeared to understand that the time of comfort and plenty was at hand, and they browsed, and stared, and ate cheerily, with nothing to excite them save the necessity of making an occasional spiteful flick at some fly which already hinted at the crowd of its fellows that would soon bear it company.

The Marchesa, Kerinveau, and the youthful heir were abroad; Ingha and Marie had pleaded to be allowed to remain all winter at the Castle to pursue their studies. It was imperative that the mother and child should pass the cold weather in a warm climate, and the Marchesa, having found herself baffled for the nonce by her daughter's determination, gladly devoted her attention to her delicate son.

The girls had not been disappointed with their quiet season; their immunity from social distractions had been most welcome; time never lacked employment for either, and often Marie would go for long rambles alone to the places whose dear associations were known to none but Archie and herself, though she never passed under the beeches without self-reproach and shame. She would fain have told Ingha of that one night's folly and bliss which the proximity of those trees recalled; she would gladly have relieved her heart of the burden that memory had become, but a proud reticence sealed her lips, and, notwithstanding her regret, she was waiting in hope. No one but Ingha suspected that she really loved Archie; the Marchesa had long ago forgotten even her assumptions on the subject.

The sky was soft blue to the utterest horizon, flecked by fleecy, white clouds; a thousand ripples glistened on the loch, and the beauty of the scene was reflected on the fair faces of the two friends as they strolled by the river, their thoughts at the other side of the world. Neither felt it necessary to keep up any semblance of interest in conversation—blessed test of rare friendship!

But by-and-by Ingha broke the silence.

"What an appropriate day, Marie," she said, "for good news! I wonder if you will have any letters, and I wonder too if they have found It yet?"

"They" were their lovers, and "It" was the mythical, big, white stone which

was to send them back to love and congenial work.

"It" was as much a household word
with the girls as it was to all who worked
at the Diamond Fields; scores of diggers
there believed themselves predestined to
find It, and many a penniless group held
long and serious consultations about their
plans for the future after becoming the
actual possessors. All agreed that the stone
must not be parted from at the Fields; the
tender-conscienced, incorruptible agents
of the European diamond merchants were
to receive the haughty go by; the courteous, versatile Count who was told every-
one's secrets, though he never was known
to seek such confidences, nor to betray a

trust, in this chimerical case, was to be specially shunned, and all brokers, " kopje walluppers," and buyers were to be treated with the stinging indifference that many a hard and one-sided bargain merited.

One condition was usually spoken of, but always assented to without argument because of its extremely prodigal proportions. The lucky finder of the new kooinoor was appointed to go immediately after unearthing It to Capetown, of course accompanied by a troop of his vagabond, well wishing friends, and there to charter the best of Donald Currie's steamers to take the trip to England. What was afterwards to happen was generally so diversified by discussion as to be utterly unintelligible. I have never read any record of this wanton and oft-planned cruise, so I conclude that the monster diamond, which has served for an illusive *ignis fatuus* to innumerable believers in luck, still lies undiscovered amid the hidden treasures of the world.

"If they find one stone," said Marie, after a pause, "you may be sure they will wait for a second, but sometimes I fear Ruy and I are not Dame Fortune's favourites. I have given up expecting any surprising gift from her, and will be quite content if she will not altogether turn her back on us."

"Ah, Marie you have never reached

down to the bottom of Pandora's box," answered Ingha. "Now I would rather believe, looking at this fair scene, that gladness is universal to-day; thoughts of suffering always jar, however glorious are the surroundings. Who knows but our noble exiles may be already on the homeward voyage, Mistress Marie, laden with the spoils of the Fields of Africa?"

"Ingha dear, I wish I had your spirit," returned her friend; "the loveliness here is always full of sadness to me."

Why should she not be sad? That same hour at the other side of the world, a once stalwart and manly form lay helpless and dying, and, in his delirium, he cried:

" A coranach, Marie ; play a coranach before it grows too dark."

Ay, that will be the appropriate music for her by and by, bitter wailing for him who shall never return, and yet his voice, with its ominous bidding, cannot reach her, she only hears a dull echo of the coranach of her weary fate. And wherefore should she not be sad, and weep ? Are not tears as profitable as smiles ? and are not all moods which have not tears, untrue to the great facts of life and to the mysteries of death ?

But the sweet springtide gave no warning, though the days were wearing on to the coming of the sorrow.

It was evening. Marie was gazing wistfully over the landscape, but her thoughts were not bounded by the limits of the scene; her book lay unread on her knee. Ingha had been singing, singing of love, constancy, and joy, and then of loss, and grief, and dole, and anon there arose a strain of hope, strong and eager, sudden as a rift in a blackened sky which discloses the moon and stars in still splendour. This priestess of song could sway the heart by the purity and power of her tones; she had made her one talent into ten, and her skill was as unerring as the divinity of her gift was sure. Only the intensest sympathy with its melody and impulse could have given her the feeling with which she sang Mendelssohn's Spring song, sweetly and rapturously for very gladness in the praise with which it is replete.

Till the crisis of life be passed, till the laurel wreath be lost, the idol broken, or the seeming rock under our feet has proved but a landslip, music suggests dreams that are full of vague beauty all of future joy; afterwards it moans to us only of the past, and is merciful in making us weep.

A message was brought to Marie that Mrs. Campbell had called and wished to see her. Marie hurried to her, hoping and yet dreading; one glance at Mathilda's face was enough; traces of tears were on the usually calm features, and there was a tremor in her voice as she endeavoured to speak without emotion.

"Marie, we have a letter from Ruy," she said, "telling us Archie is ill, very ill."

Marie grew deadly pale as she clasped her hands tightly together. These sudden heart chills, how they shorten the lives of us all! We laugh in gay unconsciousness of pain or heart-throbbing till some stunning blow falls, and then a great thud seems to overcome us; instead of realizing the tidings that have started the throbbing, we have recourse to physical tricks to enable us to bear the inward beating. We clasp our hands together or wring them in despair, and our eyes grow dim and our cheeks grow pale, though not because of age; time is not always the influence that blanches the colour and bows the frame. I have seen a woman of eighty years whose fresh loveliness a girl might envy, but life had ever been a velvet sward to her tread. I know another face which the lily for whiteness alone can rival, but its pallor came in an evil hour. A brave English officer was assegaied in sight of his youngest born, and the horror paled the little one's cheek so that the bloom never came back to it in all the aftertime.

"Did you bring Ruy's letter?" asked Marie, hardly yet sure of the meaning of Mathilda's words.

"Yes, I did bring it, dear, but it has no comfort for any of us."

Mathilda had drawn Marie to a couch, and had put her arm round the girl's form. She had been devising brave comfort for her husband all the afternoon, but in presence of Marie's mute sorrow her solace failed; she had nerved herself to come and break the tidings, and had thought of so many hopes to express, but they all vanished from her memory, and she could do nothing but offer the letter, which Marie took, and, turning away, said:

"I will read it alone, if you will leave it with me."

"Stay, Marie, my child," said her friend, "remember you are not the only Mont-

gomerie to whom sorrow has come. Try
to be brave and worthy of your name, my
poor darling."

Marie went silently from the room, but
her white, white face, it haunted Mathilda
all through the dreary watches of that
night. And this was the message which
the bright spring days had been hurrying them to meet :

"Pniel, April 10th.

" My dear Friends,

"If I knew how to make my
news less sorrowful, God knows there is
nothing I would not sacrifice to do so.
Our poor Archie is very ill, so ill that I
cannot leave him for an hour. He has

c 2

had a sunstroke, which has been followed by fever, and he has but rare intervals of consciousness. It is eight days since I found him in this state, and the doctors give very little hope of his recovery. I am almost heart-broken, and I do not know what to say to comfort you.

"In his delirium I have heard that which makes me ask you to tell Marie of his danger gently. God help us all!

"Yours,

"Roy."

CHAPTER II.

THE BITTERNESS OF DEATH.

He'll ride nae mair to meetin' fair,
  He'll gae nae mair to kirk nor ha';
Ah! weel I mind the very birds
  Sang douce the day he gaed awa'!

And a' the folk, baith high and low,
  Are greetin' sair, like bairnies sma';
For in their hearts the lad did bide,
  E'en tho' sae far he gaed awa'.

TEN long, weary days had to elapse ere further tidings could arrive, and Marie's unconcealed indifference to passing

events during the time frightened Ingha, though she was advised by Mistress
Gilroy not to disturb this communion
of sorrow. Coyla knew so many of the
aspects which grief wears, had herself
walked hand in hand with it, slept with
its cruel face on her pillow, and waked to
find it constant and abiding.

The return of the Marchesa and Kerinvean had been deferred until June, and
for this respite Ingha felt relief on Marie's
account. The evenings were very dull
now, but Ingha tried to express her sympathy through her art, she knew no better
way ! She essayed all the strains she
knew Marie loved, but in vain; for the
poor girl sat for hours idle and listless,

with not even the pretence of reading, her hands clasped, and her head slightly bent forward, as if listening for a step or a voice beyond her hearing.

Ingha's love was pitiful, and she tried to devise how to make the hours pass quickly, but her efforts were fruitless, and daily Marie's anxiety and terror showed more plainly. With great tenderness, Ingha sang in these days, and often her voice sounded like that of a mother crooning lullabys over her sick child, but, alas! there was no response in Marie's heart. She was on the eve of the crisis of her fate, and she foresaw too plainly the bitterness of the morrow.

In the years while the Possible is still

limitless, music's deepest pathos has hints
of hope, strains that rend the measures to
bless us with visions of coming joy, and
all melodies are but songs of the rapture
and the love to which we are hastening.
Music opens to us the gate of our Eden,
and its magic and mystery lull us into
dreams wherein we see the glory that
lies beyond. In the aftertime, when we
have realized how deep is the suffering
of which the human soul is capable, have
drank perchance to the dregs the cup of
love and sorrow, the change then comes.
The old spells are powerless to make us
hope; we listen, but, ah, me! it is no
longer ours to be lured into enchanted
palaces, the gardens of the Hesperides are

watched by the sleepless dragon; we hearken, but the strains are all dirges, even a Bacchic chorus falls on our spirits like a wail. Where is the ancient charm? The skilled hand still wields the bow, and the strings are in perfect tune; but our day of grace is over, and the gate that led to our Paradise is fast closed, and for this human life there is no blissful to-morrow.

Sometimes Marie's thoughts shaped themselves into a prayer, and then would recur with a pang of despair the dread that perhaps this was now useless for Archie. She had always believed that it was bootless to plead for the soul that had gone to "the mercy of the merciful," but her passionate grief sought to scale the impenetrable wall that has affrighted so many stricken ones whose anguish was already overwhelming. Marie had never before been perplexed by this subject, but, like others tempted to the uttermost, she put aside her belief as an inheritance from Puritan fear, and she condoned her present conviction, thinking that, in the dark ages when truth was assailed on all sides, the Puritan rebound from error made such strongholds necessities, and, when the brave band came to be framers of a creed, one of their chief designs had evidently been to make it in every particular the antithesis of that held by their enemies.

At length the mournful tidings arrived, the tidings of Archie's death, and sore indeed was many a heart which held no memory of him that was not bright and kindly. It was from Sir Dallas that the news came, and Mathilda sent the letter at once to Ingha, whose dread for the safety of her own love helped her to realise and to minister to her desolate friend.

When Ingha went to Marie's room, the poor girl looked into her face with a terrified hopelessness, and, seeing the sad truth written there, she flung her arms above her head and wrung her hands in agony.

" Oh, Archie, Archie, my Love, my

Love! where are you?" she moaned, as she sank down in a merciful swoon.

Ingha chafed her temples and her hands, but the eyes and lips remained fast closed; presently, however, a deep-drawn sob, and consciousness, and then again she moaned:

"Where are you, my Darling?"

In the first despairing moments of bereavement, the soul stands aghast in its solitude. The lonely, unspeakable bewilderment, and the terrible, unutterable dread of an eternal separation, take possession of the mind which staggers in the darkness, sending the yearning and pathetic cry after the spirit of the departed: "Where are you, my Darling?"

"Oh! Marie, Marie, you know, you know!" said Ingha, whose tears fell fast and whose words were few.

"Yes; but my Love, my Love!" the poor girl sobbed.

No shame now that death had stolen her Beloved; he was her dead by right of the supremacy of grief. Ay, and he too had claimed her on that death-bed. Not much comfort, poor, broken heart! but those who are predestined to sorrow have to stoop to the earth for the waters of healing. The streamless, shadeless desert is the appointed way, trackless and lonely, the valley of the shadow of Death must be crossed, and the soul's best beloved lost in its mists; then blessed are they who, through their tears, see one like the Son of Man lighting up its gloom, for the road that leads on and on will be no less desolate and lonely, till the infinite sea of eternity looms in sight, and the end, which is merely the beginning, is reached at last.

CHAPTER III.

FORECAST.

"   .   .   .   As one who is impatient
To see what it behoves him to escape,
And whom a sudden terror doth unman,
Who, while he looks, delays not his departure."

                    TRANSLATION FROM DANTE.

SIX weeks had passed since Archie was buried at Klipdrift, and still Dallas Gore lingered on the banks of the Vaal. For many days Ruy had been very ill, but at length the vigorous constitution asserted itself, and he was now convalescent and capable of work. Gore and he were sitting one evening in the house reading, when the former looked up from his book, and said:

" Have you made up your mind to go with me, Montgomerie?"

"You are very good to care about having me, but I'm sure I could not get through even a month of idleness just now. I remember days that were never half long enough for the loafing I could do in them, but it was the river and hills of Kerinveau that were responsible, but now I feel it is imperative on me to work."

" I understand that perfectly; but if

you went with me to the Zambesi you might turn 'smouse,' and barter when opportunity occurred, and shoot for the sake of the value of the spoil, and sketch subjects for future works of art. My waggon and oxen will do as well for two as for one, and you will be certain to like the reality of it all better than you like the prospect of it here. You could trust Howes or Dick to work the claim on half shares, and we'd call at New Rush on our way down country; I don't want to leave you here."

"Gore, it won't do," answered Ruy, " nor do I mean to remain at the Fields after you go. I could not stay on here now; when you leave, 1 leave too. The

claim is yielding splendidly, but the luck
began too late. Already I have value to
a larger amount than I brought out. If I
have a thousand pounds clear when I
return to England I shall not be badly off,
for I have gained something in experience besides. We had ambitions once
that it would have taken all the yields of
New Rush Kopje to satisfy, and with him
I could have been content to wait till they
were fulfilled; but stay here without him,"
and Montgomerie looked round the little
place, shook his head hopelessly and added,
" no, it's impossible."

" But what do you mean to do
at home?" asked Gore, somewhat perplexed.

" To work, of course ; I always meant this
to be the preliminary of an art career. I
hoped to be lucky, to insure myself against
the temptation of mingling mercenary
motives with my work. I had odd notions
of being independent of the fruits of my
labours in art, but those have been modified. I know now how sickening it is to
work with no returns, and, so long as the
world gauges a man's power by his success, I suppose there will always be a
crush to the front to hear the result of the
bidding. I have given myself five years
wherein to study, and I expect I shall
learn a little more about my own audacious ignorance during that time, and
perhaps at the end of it I may be able to

D 2

do a little towards my own mainte-
nance."

"But, meantime, how do you intend to
live ?" asked Gore.

"You are forgetting my thousand ; it
will yield me two hundred per annum for
five years. I am not going to invest the
money, but live on the capital." Ruy said
this with a smile that was melancholy
enough to preclude Gore joining it, and
added, "As Montgomerie, Younger of
Kerinvean, that would have been an indifferent income, but, as an obscure student, I shall have no temptation to prodigal habits. My sister has our mother's
small fortune, but in any case we could
not live together, it would be unspeakably

lonely for her; I shall take no respite till I have accomplished, or—failed."

" I fear," said Gore, after a pause, "you will never effect anything; with such a pittance how can you procure even materials and instruction? I wish you would borrow from me and pay me back in pictures."

" I promise you one thing, Gore, I will never borrow from anyone else; but I think, with my present ideas, I can manage very well. The hardier my life, the better I believe it will be for my work. I might stay on for a while longer here and lose all I have got; digging is like gambling, there is the same excitement winning or losing, and the same eagerness for the

next chance, and one goes on and on and
may throw away everything; besides, you
know I must go home and face them all
without him, and that is heavy on my
mind; my sister's grief is the trouble
about which I am constantly thinking."

"Montgomerie," Gore began, hesitatingly, "Archie gave me a message for
your sister; do you advise me to write it
to her, or to wait till I return to England?
I have tried to word it in a letter, but I
think it is more difficult for me than it
would be for anyone else."

"Why?" asked Ruy, who had not once
recalled the episode of Archie's delirium
after Gore's arrival.

"Because I left England to try if other scenes would make me forget her, for I knew she loved him, though she did not know I cared for her."

Ruy was greatly astonished, but answered :

"I must have been intensely wrapped up in my own concerns, for I never suspected anything about either him or you of this kind, and I imagine Archie and Marie could not have altogether concealed their feelings."

"I don't know," answered Gore. "My own impression is that Flash had some Quixotic notions about not being her equal after he lost his fortune, but this is mere supposition."

"He was more eager than anyone I ever knew to succeed," said Ruy, "and his belief in ultimately doing so was an enthusiasm that never flagged. He had spirit enough to accomplish anything. It would give Marie more comfort, I think, if you told her Archie's message, than if you wrote it. You will return soon, I hope?"

"I do not know, and sometimes I care as little," answered Sir Dallas.

Ruy knew the fascination of the life of wandering and sport in which his friend had chosen to try to forget the scenes he had left behind. Long solitary days in which no note of time is taken, save the sun's rise and setting; the gipsy roaming, whose quaint, primitive habits become so soon second nature; the uninterrupted freedom, the undisturbed loneliness, the exhilarating variety of scene, these are the monopolies of the ideal Bohemian, be he sportsman or explorer. Two, three, and four years pass in even African solitudes, and one comes back to civilization to hear of governments tottering, armies annihilated, of innumerable social changes, and then one knows how long the absence has been, and perhaps feels a qualm of remorse at having had no responsibility in these gigantic plots, though they may seem sometimes worthy of a race of manikins, after an uninterrupted study of God's work.

The nomad life increases in fascination as the years increase. I recall one whose experiences were rare. We were up country, where Chum and I did not consider it safe to sleep without our revolver loaded and at hand, for we might (I might, certainly not you, Chum!) have mistaken the approach of a foe for the laughing bark of the jackal, which was our usual nightly serenade, and this Bohemian, an astronomer, outspanned not far from us, and we offered him the hospitality of our lodge, begging him to stay as protection, but he smiled as he told me he would be "there if needed," but that he could not contemplate taking rest under a roof, as he had never essayed doing so except on two occasions during the last twelve years! The very defencelessness of his waggon was its chief security, he had got used to sleeping lightly, "on a nerve," he described it, and he never liked to leave the companionship of his precious astronomical instruments. This individual had had the highest English educational and social advantages, but the love of exploring had become so engrossing that nothing would ever supplant it.

"So you do not mean to come with me, Montgomerie?" said Gore, later on the same night. "And you are going to work, and I to play!"

"Oh, you will have your innings by-and-by; it's your turn to pot the buffalo and wildebest now, but I daresay you will have a different sort of shooting and more invincible foes when the time comes."

Was he foretelling of Isandhlwana, Ghinghelovo, Intombi, and Zlobane? I trow not. We did not then suspect that the power of the sudden surprise, the rapid Herculean embrace of the horse-shoe manœuvre, and the determined advance, culminating in the last resolute rush and wild assegai thrust of the bravest troops in the world, would ever be turned against us, for many of them were then our faithful and industrious allies. No one thought, as those fellows were heard chanting time to their regular step, as they returned nightly from the kopjes at the Diamond Fields, that their tuneful voices would ever be raised into demoniac war-whoops for our intimidation, that the soft pad of their footsteps would change its fleet lightness into stealthy scouting of us, their enemies, though no one who has lived amongst Zulus ever doubted that they had unequivocal qualities for the making of warriors, and their military reverses have left no record of flinching nor lack of pluck.

Methinks the brain that devised a campaign against these noble savages, for which we were unprepared, had never seen a Zulu war-dance nor a review of Zulu troops; or, if he had, his discern-

ment of the capacity of their fighting
powers was certainly shortsighted. Alas!
for these poor fellows, though heroic en-
durance and magnificent manœuvring were
all in vain against Martini-Henris, grape-
shot, and Gatlings, yet deeds of valour were
performed by these barbaric battalions
which amazed and startled the world.
No white feather there, as the heaps of
our noble slain testify, only the Sakubula,
the crimson war-token, which, alas! alas!
was daringly flaunted to the death-dealing
muzzles of our English guns.

CHAPTER IV.

MONTGOMERIE TURNS HIS BACK ON CHANCE AND LUCK.

" He went, and turned not. From his shoes
It may be that he shook the dust,
As every righteous dealer must
Once and again ere life can close :
And unaccomplished destiny
Struck cold his forehead, it may be."

D. G. ROSSETTI.

MONTGOMERIE had wisely determined to sell his finds in London, for temerity in speculation was now banished

from the Diamond Fields, and in its place
an excessive caution prevailed. Not long
after the discovery of the New Rush (Kim-
berley) mine, the fall in the market com-
menced; there followed fluctuations, but
a slow and steady decrease in prices con-
tinued, from which there was no permanent rise. This was partly attributable to
the immense number of large off-coloured
stones for which too high prices had been
given in the early days, and also because
the merchants had already embarked
almost the whole of their floating capital
in stones which could not be quickly
enough got ready for the trade, the art
of diamond-cutting being confined to a
limited number who hold it as a monopoly,

to which money will not avail to secure an apprenticeship.

Certainly never in the world's history has there been such a demand for brilliants as during the last ten years. Indian princes, always preferring treasure to capital, are still as rapacious for amassing gems as they were in the days before the storming of Delhi, in which stronghold they had stored such priceless loot for British hands. Increased population of the wealthy mercantile class, who spend as well as accumulate, and who consider any occasion for family presentations reason sufficient for diamond-buying ; but, notwithstanding, the digger rarely benefits from these broader facts.

Montgomerie's house sold for two hundred pounds, and his claim was put into the hands of the literary local auctioneer, who advertised it for disposal in the popular newspaper of the district.

The fact of the auctioneer and the owner of the newspaper being one and the same person, and that that person included the personality of another hypothetical person, who was reported to be retained to compose advertisements at an impossibly high salary, which advertisements had to be paid for by the victims who needed that channel of celebrity, had, of course, no weight in lengthening those productions, the literary and auctioneering mind being incorruptible and undefiled. No dictation nor interference was permitted by the editor, who was responsible for the following, which appeared in very large and varied type in his valuable columns:

ARREST YE, WEARY DIGGERS!

Come to "The Blue Post," at Twelve o'clock,

On Thursday!

To be Sold, for an old Song,

THE RIVAL OF GOLCONDA!

No. 22 Claim, at present owned by

RODERIGUE MONTGOMERIE, ESQUIRE.

It has been very little worked, and towers head

and shoulders above its surroundings,

like its Owner!

This Claim is chock full of Kooinoors, and it is

here that the

BIG STONE!!!

Will be found, though its fortunate possessor has

expectations of a less exciting nature

IN EUROPE,

E 2

Where our good wishes will follow him ;

And he has determined to allow his friends at the

DIAMOND FIELDS

To profit by his departure, by offering the

SALE BY AUCTION

Of this unparalleled Claim, which will make

A MILLIONAIRE !!!

Of the pluckiest Bidder.

Now that the Sand Vein has been successfully run

through, and the

REFUSE CLEARED AWAY !!

It only awaits Buckets and Enterprise to carry off the

INNUMERABLE SPARKLING GEMS ! !

That lie secluded in the Maiden Blue beneath !

The claim sold for three hundred pounds, and the day after the auction, a week subsequent to Roy's abandonment of it, an eighty carat perfect stone was unearthed there—the luck again too late !

Ruy went before leaving the Fields to pass an hour at Archie's grave, and to spend a night at Pniel. Arriving at Mrs. Quarrier's, the good woman received him kindly as ever, but her face was expressive of concern.

"I've found my Jack at last, Mr. Montgomerie, but he's ailing and is in the room at the end of the stoop, my best room."

"I'm glad to hear you have found him after all," returned Ruy; "any place will do for me; I leave very early in the morning. If you can give me a stretcher, and will tell Nestling to come to me at five o'clock, that will be all I shall need."

Mrs. Quarrier showed him into a little

place beyond her "best room;" between the two there was only a thin partition, which was by no means proof against sound.

Ruy bade her good night and shut the door, but, though tired, sleep would not come. Footsteps of customers, nightly visitors going in and out the canteen, familiar sounds and tones which re-called many an association, kept his mind wakeful, and Chum too was alert though still, as was his habit on the eve of a move.

"Mother, mother," cried a querulous voice, interrupted by coughing.

" Yes, Jack; I'm coming directly with your tea. Are you better?" asked the soothing tones of Mrs. Quarrier.

"I'm middling," answered the querulous voice.

A few minutes after, the tea and toast having doubtless had a pleasing effect, the voice resumed :

"I've been a bad lot, mother."

"Yes, you have, Jack," said the truthful woman ; "but you're going to mend now, and we'll be ever so comfortable together; you see if you don't, you've the makings of a bad old man in you yet."

"I don't know as I should much care about mending and coming it good," went on the querulous Jack ; "good people are such hypocrites, and, if I joined them, I'd never get another lark as long as I lived."

"They wouldn't have you unless you repented," answered Mrs. Quarrier, in an earnest tone. "You've been the worst of prodigals, Jack, for you've sinned against God, and Queen, and country, and parents as well; but you'll be forgiven, my lad; your mother ain't a-going to turn her back on her only child, and God ain't a-going to do that by His son neither, and He says He came for the wicked and bad uns as everybody else had scorned, and you are one of them, Jack, for a deserter is the most disgracefulest man in the whole service."

"Out of it, you mean, mother," put in

Jack. "I wish you'd forget I ever was a trooper; you'll be having a squad of them after me in no time."

"Oh dear, no!" said the mother, "you're too ill; and, besides, we're never going to part any more, and now you've left your evil ways you'll be far happier than you ever was."

"I don't agree with you, mother. You see you only know one side, and you haven't the ghost of a notion of the ins and outs of a real spree."

"No, I haven't," said the mother, apologetically, "but you'll tell me everything by-and-by; and now you'd better try to sleep, and I'll be within hearing if you feel bad."

A little later Ruy heard Nestling go into the invalid's room.

" Well, Jack, and how are you to-night?" he asked, kindly.

" Better, thank you, and I'm coming it John Bunyan and the ' Pilgrim's Progress.' I'm getting on. She preaches regular, and it ain't her fault if I don't turn Methody."

" You don't know what a good mother you have, Jack," said Nestling, timidly.

" I ought to," Jack answered, " only she expects too much from the likes of me, but she's good enough as mothers go, and I s'p'ose she means to do the correct thing by me, for all she's so taken up with religion."

Ere long the voices and footsteps ceased, and Ruy at last fell asleep, but wakened early to hear old Nestling pacing the verandah, where he had waited all night, fearing to be late in the morning.

Mrs. Quarrier's parting was full of tears, and when she held Ruy's hand many unspeakable thoughts came into both their minds.

" Good-bye, Nestling," said Ruy. " We'll all meet again some time, I trust."

" I feel sure we shall meet again, Mr. Montgomerie," answered the old man, his dignity struggling hard with his feelings, "how or where the Lord only knows, but I shall never cease to hope for it."

And, as Ruy drove up the Pniel road, he saw little Nestling, who was being ferried across the Vaal in the golden sunrise; he was standing in the boat bareheaded, waving his hand. It was meet to leave him in the sunrise, for the dawn of an eternal day could not be far off from that dauntless and gentle soul.

CHAPTER V.

"O YOU MUST WEAR YOUR RUE WITH A DIFFERENCE."

MONTGOMERIE did not arrive in England until two months after the tidings of Archie's death had been received at Kerinvean; he waited a week in London, where he sold his diamonds for nine hundred pounds, and then started on his sad errand.

It was not unexpected at Invean that he

should propose to go there instead of to the Castle. Marie had been invited to stay with Mrs. Campbell while Ingha went to meet her mother in town, where they were to remain a month.

Ingha had more than one reason for regret on parting from Marie; she feared that by the time the Kerinvean household should have returned Ruy would no longer be at Invean, and an indefinable dread that she would not see him saddened her; and bitter it seemed to her that the once-recognized heir should be coming back to no welcome, and not even to the hospitality of his old home.

It was a sorry meeting for Ruy; each one in the quiet Invean family circle felt that the vacant place of the beloved son could never be filled again, and that to all of them his loss was irreparable. Ruy had much to tell of Archie, and, after a time, their life at the Fields became a subject which at least proved a link to the past.

The first wild bitterness of Marie's grief was over, she never spoke of Archie to anyone, but between Mr. Campbell and herself had sprung up a strong sympathy, born of the sorrow that has robbed life of its hope. The father's loss was profound, but not so selfish as to render him indifferent to the speechless patience of the girl's face, and a tender pity for his son's beloved showed in all his intercourse with her.

Marie realised to the full now that she must take up her life without the dear hope that had lent all the glory she had foreseen in the future. She knew she should meet her lover here no more, that never again should they stand in rapture like that they had known in the brief hour under the quiet stars, when he had claimed her for eternity; and an unspeakable yearning for the hereafter took possession of her. But Death opens not the portal for mere pleading. " One shall be taken, the other left," is a stern and mysterious fiat which knows no abrogation.

Ruy gave Archie's stone to his sister, and told her everything which he thought

could comfort her, and delivered a letter
which Sir Dallas Gore had given to his
care when they parted. It contained only
these few words :

" DEAR MISS MONTGOMERIE,

"Not daring to intrude
my sympathy upon you now, I wish
merely to tell you of a sacred message
entrusted to me. Archie's words were :
'Tell her I never forgot. I know
we shall meet again!' What there is
of comfort in this, God grant you
find !

" DALLAS GORE."

Ruy had no heart to go to any of his
old haunts, he had never more keenly

realised the loss of his comrade than now, and he felt he could not bear to stay long in the place where he heard constantly the echoes of Archie's voice, and the ring of that laughter the spell of which even the gravest had ever been unable to resist.

Old Peter was in a very feeble state of health, and Ruy soon went to visit him.

"So I've lived to bid ye welcome, Master Ruy," said the old man in greeting, "the Lord has given me my heart's desire. You have come back yer lane, and, oh, the place is sair changed."

Ruy pressed his hand, and answered :

" Yes, we are all changed, Peter,
but I don't see any difference in the
place."

" No, there's no that difference in God's
wark, the fulishness is a' our ain, but
it'll a' be richt ae day. Ye are na gaen
awa' ony mair ?"

" No, not far, Peter—only to London,
or somewhere within call, to my work."

" Wark! wark! Is there no wark
eneugh here for ye? Tak' awa' Kerinvean and twal mile round, and whar are
ye? What for should ye gang frae
Kerinvean ?"

"For good work, I hope, Peter; you wouldn't have me stay here now?"

"Wad I no?" responded the old man, eagerly. "Ye wad never gae farther than the Kerinvean marches could I keep ye here; but there's folk that think they ha'e mair richt to bide, an' we maun submit. · But, Master Ruy,"—Peter's eyes grew bright and his voice a degree stronger,—"ye'll get a salmon doon by the Black Fir the nicht; the new keeper will be in's bed; my fly-buik's on the shelf there. Hist ye, and I'll gi'e ye the ane the fish canna refuse."

Ruy could not forbear a smile to see how absorbing the ruling passion still was as the feeble old man tried to raise him-

self, pointing to the shelf on which his
fly-book rested.

"Peter, you wouldn't like me to be
taken for a poacher; the river will never
be mine, and I would not care to fish in
it without you, so don't look for flies to-
night."

But Peter was ill-comforted, and seemed
perplexed between desire and duty; and,
after some conversation about Ruy's
travels and his own illness, Ruy wended
his way back to Invean.

The reserve in which Ruy hid all his
deeper feelings hindered him from encouraging either Mathilda or Marie to
speak of Ingha. He asked no questions about her, though his cravings for

tidings were painful, and there were times when the experiences he had so lately gone through weighed upon his spirits so much that his hopes seemed to elude him.

Marie was perplexed; the shipwreck of her own happiness gave her a keen foresight of the storms that threatened the horizons of those whom she loved, and she pondered much how to avert them. But Ruy never hinted a word about Ingha's existence, and in these days Marie was easily daunted and mistrustful of herself.

About a fortnight after Ruy's return, he received the following letter:

" Kerinvean Castle.

" MY DEAR RUY,

"I have come from London specially to see you on urgent business. Will you come here to-day to talk over matters with me? Kindest regards to all.

" Yours sincerely,

" STEUART MONTGOMERIE."

A somewhat undutiful impulse prompted an excuse, but his wiser feelings prevailed, and, not greatly troubling himself with conjectures, Ruy started off at once, followed by Chum. He sauntered across the fields, and through the woods, which seemed to be even yet waving the same welcome to him that he had ever found in the past ; nor did he love them one whit less now that the possibility of possession was a memory that never troubled his brain.

CHAPTER VI.

RELINQUISHED, BUT NOT FREE.

"But in my spirit will I dwell,
 And dream my dream, and hold it true;
 For though my lips may breathe adieu,
 I cannot think the thing farewell."

TENNYSON.

O N arriving at his old home, Ruy was
informed that Kerinvean had gone
out, but had left word that he would return in an hour. Ruy told the footman,

who was a stranger to him, that he would wait in the library.

The man stared as the visitor walked into the hall, and, drawing aside a tapestry portière, passed through an arch into the gallery, the longest way to the library.

"That is the gallery, the picture-gallery," volunteered the astonished servant, who was following him.

"Tell Kerinvean that Mr. Roderigue Montgomerie waits for him."

"I beg your pardon, sir," returned the footman. "I hought to have perceived you was one of the family."

Ruy went on, looking at the familiar pictures and at the old armour, every curve and dent of which he knew so well.

He sighed as he recalled how often Archie
and he, when boys, had eluded everybody
for the sake of donning these suits, how
they were wont to copy the portraits with
their helmets, and greaves, and gauntlets,
and how once Archie—"Ah, there was
the very breastplate and dagger,"—put on
a most elaborate coat of mail, much too
large for his then slender figure, and the
old butler came suddenly upon them, and
Archie darted against the unsheathed
misericorde Ruy held, and was pierced by
it on the shoulder; but he laughed when
the blood oozed out, and only said :

"When I'm dead, Rue, I'll get credit for
this wound, and, considering it's in front,
they can't call me coward !"

Other memories crowded in Ruy's brain as he sauntered on, Chum at his heels, but he was arrested suddenly by a new picture, hung opposite the stove over which Sir David Montgomerie looked mournful as of yore.

Ruy was fascinated, gladdened, ay, thrilled in every pulse.

"And they have put you among the Montgomeries, my star! a fair, sweet sarcasm, my queen of them all! a radiant Peri in a court of mummies!" he said, half aloud, while gazing hungrily at the face which had haunted his dreams for upwards of two long, dreary years.

It was Iugha, in her lovely womanhood, smiling, gracious, and of a noble bearing,

but Ruy yearningly sought for that which
the portrait lacked. The features were
exquisitely painted, the pose was perfect
serenity, the dress and surroundings were
superb. She was standing in an Eastern
court, and all about her were groups of
palms and tropical flowers, and she was
the fairest flower of all, but the wistful
enthusiasm which pervaded Ingha's nature
and showed so constantly in her expression was not indicated in the portrait, and
yet that alone would have rendered any
features beautiful, and would have been
inspiration enough for a higher work of
art.

"Your face is here, my star, but your
soul did not look out of your eyes on

him who painted this picture. One
day, if God wills, I will prove more
faithful."

And Ruy turned away and saw that
Chum had ensconced himself in a favourite alcove where they had often spent
hours together, Ruy drawing and Chum at
his side asleep; but Chum was not sleeping now, his chin was on his fore paws,
and he was eagerly watching Ruy and
the picture; he had evidently gone to the
alcove to leave Ingha and his master
undisturbed.

"Come along, Chum; you are too familiar here, my dog."

Ruy now opened the library door, and
Kerinvean's staghound rose on hearing

an intruder, and came on as if for victory.

"Lie down, Chief," said Ruy, but the hound was baying with delight, and pawed and licked Ruy to such a degree that Chum could not forbear one little, sharp bark of jealousy, whereupon Chief turned round and gave Chum a fraternal lick, but turned again to Ruy with the demonstrative welcome that only the reserved by nature ever offer with pleasing effect.

Ruy had not long to wait, and, when he heard Kerinvean's step, he went forward to greet him.

"How are you, my boy?" said his uncle, shaking his hand warmly. "Very glad you escaped sunstroke, and fevers, and snake-bites. I am rejoiced to see you here again."

"Thank you, uncle," returned Ruy. "I am delighted to find you looking so well."

"Oh, I'm all right; I never did ail anything, you know. I wish I could say as much for the youngster, but he too is stronger since we took him abroad."

"And the Marchesa, is she well?" asked Ruy, whose courtesy never deserted him.

"Oh, yes, thanks," answered Kerinvean, in haste. "I would ask you to come and see us in town, but this blessed business about Ingha worries me terribly."

"I don't understand to what you allude," returned Ruy, in some fear.

"No, I daresay not. But sit down, Ruy. How brown you are! I wanted to ask you to take the management of the property again, but the Marchesa does not approve, says it might bring you and Ingha too much in contact, and—and—in fact—" and here Kerinvean's flow of language failed as Ruy interrupted him.

"Kerinvean, you must be under some misapprehension. I have come back to do my own work, and no inducement could make me forego it."

"Yes, yes, that's all right," returned Kerinvean, evidently at a loss to know how to introduce the real object he had had in view in seeking the conversation : "I am sure you will choose correctly, and never disgrace our name; but the Marchesa is so bent on the marriage about which I wrote to you—Lord Arthur Daneleigh and Ingha. He has begun to visit us again after we thought the intimacy between them was quite broken off; and Ingha, well, she does not seem to discourage him, in fact, quite the reverse, and the Marchesa says (how she finds things out I cannot tell, but she is a clever woman, a wonderfully clever woman) she thinks Ingha would have accepted Lord Arthur long ago, but fears there must have been some boy and girl understanding between you two, and that of course, as Ingha is romantic, she does not consider herself free. You know it would be a sad thing for her immense fortune to be thrown away, and—and, in fact—sit down, Ruy, sit down, and let us talk this matter over quietly."

Ruy rose from his chair while his uncle drivelled on; his face had flushed and his eyes had become unnaturally bright as he listened; he took no notice of Kerinvean's request that he should sit down again, but said, in a stern voice:

"I do not understand why this conversation should have taken place."

"No, of course not," answered Kerinvean, more excited and confused as he perceived his nephew's pride coming to the contest, "but you know I stand now in the place of her father, and we thought, the Marchesa thought, that, if you had any understanding with Ingha when you were my heir, it would only be just to relinquish any such claim on her now."

"This gratuitous insult is based merely on conjecture; I never had any claim save that of friendship on Miss di Garcelli," said Ruy, proudly, "and, now that I am not your heir, I relinquish even that slight bond. Is there any other *urgent business* upon which you wish to speak before I go?"

"No, Ruy, you have behaved like a

Montgomerie. Then I can tell her mother
that you will make no effort to see Ingha ?
I understand this ?"

"Understand what you choose, Kerinvean, I have nothing more to say."

And having so spoken, stung to the heart,
sorely wounded, and without reasoning
the matter, Ruy turned away, and walked
quickly out of a side entrance, followed by
Chum, down a short by-path which led to
the river.

He went on and on unthink-
ing and unheeding, his brain confused, and feeling nothing save the
blow that had been so ruthlessly
dealt.

He walked for miles up the river-side,

over rocks, and moss, and heather, through
woods and fields, obeying a necessity for
motion ; his nerves seemed on fire, and he
heeded not the distance. For many a
weary mile he trudged, but the sun was
hot, and at last he was conscious of
fatigue, so he sat down by the river, and
the " hush, hush " of hurrying waters had
the old spell over him, and he fell
asleep, and, as he slept, dreamed in this
wise :

A little skiff waited beside steep marble
steps that led to a palace, from whence it
is to take him to a ship lying out in the
bay. One last look round the eastern
court filled with tropical flowers, where

everything is still and solitary and strangely familiar in the moonlight. Suddenly, as he turns to descend the steps, the white-robed form of a maiden, radiant and smiling, appears, and pointing upwards to the sky, where but one bright star glitters in a rift of cloud, she utters, in a clear, sweet, and well-remembered voice :

"If thou thy star do follow,
    Thou canst not fail thee of a glorious port,"

and, while he is intently dwelling on the last echo of her tones, the vision vanishes as suddenly as it had appeared.

He descends to the skiff, he voyages far,

wanders through ancient cities and lonely lands, and lingers longest where Art has left her impress. Sure, like the pillar of fire by night and cloud by day, which guided the ancient Israelites, his star points always where he shall go. In every city, every land where Art has her trophies and triumphs, there be toils unwearyingly, and, though the star is not withdrawn, he seems to be ever invoking the vision which appears not again.

Years pass in the illusive world of his dream, and those years are spent in toil and thought so ardent that he seeks nothing from his fellows save liberty to fulfil; often sorely tried and discouraged, he

looks where the star should be, and it
shines the clearest when his cares beset
him most.

An hour comes when he is completing
a statue to which all his skill, all his deepest inspiration have been given; at length
he essays to rest from his labour, but his
heart still is yearning, and he needs the
incessant presence of his work to keep
up the zealous fires of his imagination.
He looks long at his statue, and then turns
to gaze out into the night. His star is
obscured, and, shuddering, he thinks this
omen presages failure.

Ah! what sees he as he withdraws from
watching the darkened sky to solace himself with his art? The figure of a lovely

woman stands beside his sculptured Priestess of Song, and bends over it weeping. He moves forward towards the maiden, who, turning to him, discloses again the vision of Ingha, and once more he hears the thrilling tones of her voice :

" Thou hast followed thy star, and gained the port; but, ah me! hast thou given all thy love to thine Art, while I have been faithful to thee alone ?"

She holds her arms out yearningly towards him; but suddenly, in the rapture of that meeting, his dream broke off. Solitary at the river side Roderigue Montgomerie was lying, and the " hush, hush " of hurrying waters was the only sound he heard.

He rose up refreshed, calm, and resolute ; whatever betided, he knew nothing could ever really separate him from Ingha, even if she herself forsook him he would love her no less ; but to divide his life's purpose from thoughts of her was utterly and for ever impossible. Whatever barriers should rise between them, while he struggled to attain, his inspiration would come from her alone, and his work and his silent devotion would be altogether dedicated to her, and perchance one day his efforts would not be scorned nor his love despised.

Ay, and meanwhile, if another claimed her, he knew the star would not even then grow dim, for it shone alone in the heaven of his desire, peerless, serene, and abiding.

CHAPTER VII.

A GRIM MAESTRO.

"Greatness in art (as assuredly in all other
things, but more distinctly in this than in most of
them,) is not a teachable nor gainable thing, but
the expression of the mind of a God-made-great
man; that teach, or preach, or labour, as you will,
everlasting difference is set between one man's
capacity and another's, and this God-given supremacy is the priceless thing, always just as rare
in the world at one time as another."

RUSKIN.

" I have some wounds upon me, and they smart
To hear themselves remembered."

SHAKESPEARE.

AND time rolled on quickly enough for
Ruy Montgomerie's work, at which,

first in Paris and then in Rome, he
toiled morning, noon, and night, with
no abatement of energy nor flagging
of care.

I do not propose, under cover of a love
story, to write even a single chapter merely on the development of power in art,
nor to propagate any heterodox theories
concerning its influence or its worship,
but I must open the studio-door to see
how this man's life purpose was attained.

Notwithstanding the lack of all external
encouragement, Montgomerie found satisfaction daily growing; not that he ever
approved of his own work, but he was
aware of a strength that was born of la-

bour, and although his own conceptions, compared with his ideal, appeared to himself like the grains of sand at the base of a Colossus, the consciousness of an increasing power rendered his life more complete. He worked in clay when daylight waned, and this was his relaxation from his easel. His studio in Rome was filled with crude, original casts and copies of the ancient sculptures.

He toiled incessantly for two years, so that, with all his previous practice and study, he was now sufficiently proficient to reproduce with great fidelity pictures and frescoes, and for these copies he found ready purchasers, though he had sternly kept a resolution of never offering for sale any conception of his own.

About this time a celebrated painter chanced to see a study Ruy had made from an almost obliterated fresco, and perceiving in it a subtle difference from the original, which foretold that the copyist would one day have a more skilful hand than he who had drawn the model, he sought the studio of the unknown Roderigue Montgomerie, and when he discovered his was no other than the stalwart form and noble face he had once seen, and since had vainly looked for, the old man's pleasure was doubled. He persuaded Ruy to give him sittings for a great historical picture which afterwards became a national possession;

and many hours were spent by these two in congenial labour. The Maestro became a great influence in Ruy's life; his house, which had once been a palace, was frequented by the most celebrated artists of Europe, as well as by the art-loving people of the western world, and he distinguished the young stranger by a familiarity which was as rare in his communion with his fellows as it was generous and wholesome.

This genius had long ago passed the rubicon of the critics, and now, had he cared to do it, could have led them, but he never patronized. Montgomerie found his counsel of infinite value, and, having asked him whether he would advise him to seek tuition from some recognized master by gain-ing admission as pupil to his studio, the old man answered warmly:

"What more can he teach thee than thou already knowest? thine own ignorance and inexperience are chiefly thine hindrances, will it aid either to pry into his failures? By work and by comparison thou wilt evolve more than thou canst ever learn from the schools. They can give thee rules by which to learn to draw, and can tell thee how to mix thy colours —in their fashion, but afterwards thou wilt see that they could not teach thee more than thou couldst have learnt working perseveringly with thy pencil alone. Thine own eye has already made thee draw correctly, and Nature will tell thee more about thy foolish mixture of colours than the schools. Thou hast youth wherewith to labour, hope to make thee diligent, and the heritages of all the ages to be thy guides. Be ever chary of teachers who do not themselves labour, for he who knows not by experience the difficulties and impossibilities, is not to be trusted about the results."

"But cowardly as the fear is," answered Ruy, "I foresee that when I put forward my own conceptions the critics will say I studied in no school, and will pass me over slightingly or in scorn."

The old man's eyes burned with sudden fire and he quickly responded :

"Hast thou then stooped so far as to

contemplate drinking from such stagnant pools? has a scare that thy work may become the prey of kites and vultures got hold on thee whom the gods have consecrated? Dost thou not know that they demolish only carrion, that the thing which has life immortal wings its way far above their ravaging swoop? If thou fear not and art true, thou wilt mount scathless. I had a son who too soon was known to them; his work was inspired, but, God in Heaven! they crucified him when they had perceived he was timorous. His hand could no more have helped doing work that proclaimed his genius, than the pencil of Michael Angelo could have been stayed when he designed the David, but

he early became the victim of the ignorant.
Ah, my young brother, keep thy heart
fixed on the serenity of the stars, not on
the din of human voices, and thy works
shall live and testify of thee when the
critics are forgotten."

"But, without their zeal, might not some
become too confident?" asked Ruy; "do
not they serve to check the too ardent
and crush the false?"

"I tell thee no, they serve but their own
occult purposes, whatever they may be.
We who work need to be ardent, what is
false will die naturally. If thou art dis-
cerning thou knowest too well wherein
thou hast failed, and also what thou, by
patience, hast attained; and if thou art

faithful thou will labour till thy faults are corrected. The contest becomes each day more unequal; on the one side Art, which from remote ages has left its impress on the world, and her children, who should study to be quiet and are only strong in silent labour. On the other side is ranged the band that is ever increasing, glib of tongue and pen, a changeful, variable throng, who, with a small element of critical acumen and emptied catacombs of Satanic audacity, handle the sacred things of Art's altar, and lash the weak ones into despair. Unheeding them, my brother, be diligent to follow none but the highest, and, if ever thou hast visions that excel, the true will honour thy work despite thine enemies.

Content thee at present reproducing the greatest creations, if imperfectly, then again and again, till thou canst do them faithfully, and anon essay thine own imaginings, and it may be thou wilt have gained, with increased facility, larger and more beatific vision."

The old Maestro's grim indifference to criticism was well known, though he rarely gave voice to such strong denunciations as these to his young friend whom many envied for the privilege of his preference. He had heard from time to time something of Ruy's career, and it had deepened his admiration for his character; he foresaw that such determined resolution and vigorous self-reliance would best develope the genius which underlay his persistent perseverance, and he had a ready sympathy for the spirit which had chosen its own flight and had not shirked the initiatory monotony of sternest labour.

The old man well knew that there are no greater diversities in any careers than in the different preparations for lives to be devoted to Art. He had seen those who had learnt from the schools everything it was possible for them to impart, and how weary had been the unlearning. And he had known others, more rare, who had to cultivate their own powers by unflagging toil and unwearied observation, who had to extract knowledge from their own repeated failures, but whose acquirement

ultimately was richer than ever it could
have become by the teaching of those
who themselves had not climbed up the
same steep paths, and he recognised
Montgomerie as belonging to this latter
band.

At length, after three years of absence
from England, Ruy decided to return and
to seek a studio for himself in London.
When he informed the Maestro of his
purpose, the old man showed visibly his
deep regret.

"Ah!" said he, "I feared thou wouldst
not long content thee away from thy
native land, and it is right that thou
shouldst return if inspiration comes to
thee freeëst under thine own skies; but, ah

me! how cold they are, and yet how lovely the maidens! Tell me, is it thy Betrothed there who recalls thee, my brother?"

"No," answered Ruy, "there is none who need me. My heart was long years ago given to one born in your own beloved Italy."

"And she, does she know that thou lovest her?"

"Yes, Maestro, but it is in vain; she is far as the stars above me."

"How can that be?" The old man's eyes were eager as he spoke. "Thine is a noble name, they tell me; thou hast Fame in thy grasp; thou art a beautiful youth. Is she blind, my brother?"

"No," said Ruy, smiling; "but it can never be, and I am content to have known the bliss of loving her without the gift of her love."

"Thou art not content," returned the Maestro; "the marks on thy brow are those of sad thought, and yet thou hast not seen the winters of thirty years. Sancta Maria! this is a poet, a Dante, an inspired. And thy Beatrice, is she beautiful?"

"Maestro, I see all women beautiful in the radiance of her loveliness, and, moreover, she is high born, gifted, and a priestess of song."

"And thou, thou who art climbing into the royal platform where only the great ones stand, dost thou willingly forego God's complete purpose for thee ?"

"Not willingly, Maestro; but I am powerless in this."

"Do another's arms enfold her?" asked the old man, persistently.

A shudder passed over Ruy which his friend perceived as he waited the answer.

"God forbid!" said Montgomerie, involuntarily.

"Ay, and thou must forbid it too!" returned the Maestro, solemnly. "She loves thee, this rare maiden. She will be thy bride when thou claimest her. Thou hast the gloom of thine own mountains in thy heart, but take courage, my brother, she waiteth for thee. Addio!"

CHAPTER VIII.

"WHAT'S PAST, AND WHAT'S TO COME IS
STREWED WITH HUSKS."

THE questions of the Maestro at their
last interview had wrung from
Ruy a confession which resulted in his
friend's clear sight perceiving a ray of
hope, but as yet it was only a trembling
glimmer.

No one but Archie would have ever

ventured to speak so openly about a subject on which he volunteered no confidences, and often as Ruy had plodded on alone and uncheered he had yearned for the ring of the manly laugh, and for the humorous, kindly, unfailing encouragement without which life had lost its young zest. The sadness of his features did not belie his feelings; Archie was not forgotten; and the strange mournfulness, that more than ever gave him resemblance to the portrait of his ill-fated ancestor, will never now leave the face of Roderigue Montgomerie.

Ingha had keenly suffered in consequence of Ruy's seeming coldness in not having sought a meeting with her on his return from Africa, and, after she had received from her mother the tidings that he had relinquished even the friendship between them, she had resolutely hidden her feelings from Marie.

For upwards of two years Ruy had not heard Ingha's name. Marie had never mentioned it in her letters, indeed, she was perplexed to know his wishes, for she had no clue to the truth.

Ingha concluded that pride was the cause of Ruy's apparent indifference, but her absolute faith never swerved, and her solace and hope lay in the fact that her lover was endeavouring to accomplish his vocation, and would one day fulfil the hint she had apprehended of his love in the past,

that was so near and yet seemed so far
away. She grew reserved, but bore her
sorrow uncomplainingly. She longed to
see her hero, waited on month after month,
year after year, faithful and fond, resolved
that nothing but his own spoken words
should ever make her free, though not
words of his from the lips of another; but
oh! Ruy never dreamed of the ceaseless
ache of those tarrying years.

At length, arriving in London, Ruy
found some rooms in Kensington, which
he furnished in a manner characteristic of
his taste, very simply, with nothing in-
congruous nor superfluous. It was here
that Sir Dallas Gore, returning with his
regiment from India, where he had

joined on leaving the Zambesi, found his friend.

"And so this art life satisfies you, Montgomerie?" asked Gore, somewhat incredulously.

"Well, on the whole, yes. It is not exciting, but there is enthusiasm in it, and immense pleasure in surmounting the difficulties," said Ruy, thoughtfully.

"Not in attacking them; you mean after they have been surmounted? I imagine toil must always be a curse, don't you?"

"I can't agree with you," responded Montgomerie. "The labour and the satisfaction are indissoluble; who can separate them ? and life is only complete when pain and pleasure are mingled."

"It strikes me your pleasure must all consist in hope," said Gore, looking round the room seeking, but finding nothing, to contradict his assertion.

"No, it does not. I am too gloomy to hope much, or to live in anything but the actual present, and I think the absorption of all my thoughts on my work may possibly bring fruition nearer than if I dissipated them in dreams; besides, the days are too short for all one plans to do, and the future is both vague and uncertain. I don't doubt that if I labour on fifty years I shall be able to paint something that may live after I am dead ; and, to come down to solid fact, I suppose an artist should have no desire nor excitement beyond that sort of anticipation."

"But, Montgomerie, surely you see some change ahead," said Gore, warmly. "It would be frightful to have nothing to contemplate between you and a dead man's fame."

"I told you, Gore, I did not dwell on that hope, it is not particularly cheerful, and I find the difficulties occupy my mind so constantly, I have not much time for anything else."

"I wish you would leave them for a while, Montgomerie, and come to Scotland with me," said Sir Dallas, in a serious voice. "The last time I tried to persuade

you to join me in an expedition I was
not successful, and I believe now you
were right; but, you have been working
so long and so hard, a holiday would
do you worlds of good. Besides I am
going to Invean, and your sister will be
there."

"I shall see her in London next season, I hope," answered Ruy. "She has
not been here since I came home, but she
is sure to come up next year."

"Montgomerie," said Sir Dallas, after
a pause, "I am going to—to try my
luck."

"Are you, Gore?" Ruy comprehended
at once to what his friend alluded, and
added, "I sincerely hope you may be suc-

cessful, but I am sure she thinks of Archie still."

"So do I," generously responded Sir Dallas. "I don't want her not to think of him, but if she would give me a chance to win my way some time, I would be content with very little from her till she could give me more. I am sure there is no treachery to Flash in speaking to her now, for I believe he contemplated it himself, after he knew I cared for her, and I don't want to supplant him. I honour your sister too much to expect that she, any more than I myself, could love another man as deeply as Archie Campbell; he was friend and brother to me."

"And to me even more!" said Ruy, mournfully.

"But still," went on Sir Dallas, "we have to live our lives; how empty and vacant mine is, I only know. If your sister could give me any hope, I would leave the service and attend to my place. I know it is my duty to look after things, and to spend some of my income on the land. What the money is accumulating for, Heaven only knows, but all I take of it is merely a tithe. Alone, life at home would be simple misery, and, if she cannot be won, the only thing I shall look for is active service; there, at least, would be excitement, and of course it would yield a sort of satisfaction to me to know that my fifteenth cousin, who should come after me, would mourn the fate of the late baronet who found his death on the field of battle !"

" I thought you remarked five minutes ago that it would be frightful to have nothing to contemplate between you and a dead man's fame, and here you are enlarging on the advantages of it in your own case !"

Ruy saw that Gore's mirth was altogether strained, and would fain have cheered him, but he dreaded saying anything which might lead him to anticipate more from Marie's decision than Ruy believed was possible.

"I wish you would change your mind and come with me, Montgomerie. Mrs. Campbell would rejoice to have a visit from you, and really I don't think you devote yourself enough to your fraternal responsibilities," said Gore, persuasively.

"Oh! but Marie understands, and is not the least exacting; besides, Invean is too near the Castle, and you will find I am not wanted in my old home. No, Gore, I can't give myself that sort of holiday yet, but when you return come and see me, and tell me how you fared; and," Ruy added, smiling, "if you can make Marie see things with your light on them, I shall rejoice with you, and somehow I think our old Archie would be on your side, if he knew!"

CHAPTER IX.

A FORLORN HOPE.

"The soul of Adonais, like a star,
Beacons from the abode where the Eternal are."
SHELLEY.

SORROW and time had wrought a change on Marie Montgomerie. She was still fair and stately, but the bright exuberance of youth and hope were gone for ever; her dark grey eyes had now the look that grief gives, as if tears fell readily, and her smile did not come as quickly as of yore. Many months of each year were spent at Invean, for she was almost as much beloved by the bereaved father as Archie himself had been, and to Mathilda she was even as a daughter.

"We are all so glad you have come back," was her welcome to Sir Dallas, though its frank sweetness showed how little she suspected his errand.

Mrs. Campbell soon divined the state of her guest's feelings, and, in a simple, serious fashion peculiar to herself, aided him, giving him opportunity of quiet, uninterrupted talks with Marie, planned with the tact that is the outcome of genuine sympathy.

One evening Sir Dallas found Marie alone in the drawing-room where she was sitting at a window, a book on her knee which she had not been reading ; she was looking out on the loch and hills with that oft-habitual gaze of listlessness and apathy. Gore walked to the window and stood opposite to her, silently absorbed in his own thoughts.

They were a goodly pair to look upon, and near them was a portrait of Archie painted when he was in his eighteenth year. Such a bright, handsome, young face, all aglow with that dauntless, gleeful smile his friends knew so well. The artist had caught the inspiration of the buoyant nature, and had painted the likeness with an expression that was quite familiar to his face after manhood.

Sir Dallas went nearer the picture and looked at it long and earnestly, and then came back and stood beside Marie.

"That portrait makes me feel a boy again ; I knew him so well in those days," he said.

The listless apathy fled from Marie's face, but the interest to which it gave place was not for the speaker, and he marked the change, but, true to his friend, he only felt the hopelessness of his own desires.

"Yes," said Marie, "he so often talked

of you, and you were quite a hero to us younger ones ; you were always such a good friend to him—to the very last," she added, her voice faltering as she tried to look up at her companion. " Your letter did comfort me more than I thought any-thing could ;" her eyelids drooped, and she nervously twisted the ring in which Archie's only white stone was now brightly gleaming.

" Have you," she said, after a pause— " have you anything to tell me of that little time when you were alone together, just before—just before Archie died ?"

" No," answered Sir Dallas, too gener-ous to make use of that last message unless despair drove him to do so; " Ruy will have told you more than I heard or saw. Ah! Marie, you had your noblest lover in him, but God knows I do not boast when I say that, since I first saw you, I have never had one thought that was not true to you. I do not ask yet for your love, but surely there is some common ground on which we can meet, if no other union be possible, then a fellowship of grief?"

Marie had become very pale; she fully comprehended that the man before her was staking his all in a sorry venture; there was no chord he touched which did not jar, till he uttered the word "grief," and then she felt his full sincerity. She also saw it in the tender expression of his dimmed eyes as he turned and moved across unthinkingly to Archie's portrait. Marie glanced up at it, and her boy-lover seemed to be smiling down upon them with a look which conveyed the thought that they could serve him now no more but by joy and love.

"Sir Dallas," said Marie, in a gentle voice, "your words have surprised me. I did not dream of this."

"Do you find anything strange in it?" he asked. "Flash and I were always on the same side, and what wonder that the same love should sway us."

"You know my story?" pleaded Marie. "I have had so little happiness, and yet in that brief past all the possibility of love seems buried, though I do not think I can ever quite lose Archie out of my life."

"I do not ask that you should; I ask no favour yet, save that you will let me be something to you, your friend, Archie's friend, anything. but do not condemn me to the drear banishment 1 have borne so many years."

"You are very generous," said Marie, "very patient, but oh, I know I can never love again."

"Ah, Marie, it seems to me sometimes as if 1 had enough love for us both, as if love would grow in your heart too had I some claim upon you. I can wait on—I have grown so used to waiting—for years, if, at the end, I may hope for something."

"I know how good you are," said Marie, sadly, "but I dare not promise even a friendship that would be worth your prizing; for, when I am alone, I never think of anyone or anything but the past, for it still fills my heart."

"Then I must give you Archie's message, Marie, for I am in sore strait, and I see my hopes fading out of my life, and I shall have nothing left, not even a past. When he was dying, some strange intuition or sympathy was given him, and, without a word from me, he divined the secret I would fain have hid, and he bade me give this message to you: 'Tell her,'

he whispered, ' I loved you.' Do not think
me cowardly for using his words to aid
my suit; you best know the meaning of
them, and I implore you to let them have
weight in your decision."

Marie covered her face all the time Sir
Dallas spoke of Archie; when he ceased,
she rose, her eyes wet with tears, and held
out her hand, and said :

" I am not worthy of your love; if I
had devotion in my will to bestow, it
should be yours, for Archie's sake; but I
have nothing, not even a hope of ever
feeling different."

And strong yearning to draw the tear-
stained face to his breast assailed him,
but he did not even kiss her hand; and yet

how often he had thought of the rapture of once enfolding that form that even in its apathy was sweeter and dearer than all the world beside, but the dying voice of her lover seemed to whisper in his ear when the temptation now was sorest: "I kissed her only once, Dal, and I have loved her all my life," and he was restrained. He held her hand a brief moment, and then with stern resolution folded his arms across his breast.

"Marie," he said, "you are going from me, but listen one moment ere you go. I think five years of faithfulness gives me some right to speak. I tell you now, whatever I do in future I do it with reference to the hope that one day you will relent; hush, dear, this is no hurried resolve, and whatever you say I cannot change it. I know that at present it is impossible for you to contemplate the thought of marriage, but I will wait on and on till one of us two shall die, loving you just the same. God knows I tried to crush my feelings when it was sin to think as I do now. Archie put the hope into my hands freely, voluntarily, and, in God's sight, he gave you to me; though you never ratify his act you cannot cancel it. I ask nothing from you yet, not even a promise that you will try to think differently, but I trust you will not banish me. I will not trouble you with my presence too frequently, and if I cannot win you,

Marie, you shall have no cause to be ashamed of the lover your coldness will doom."

But it was no fortified citadel this knightly soldier was storming, only a rudderless wreck that was drifting over the dark waters where her goodly argosy went down, and yet in his sight it was a prize whose equal he would never again behold !

She went out from his presence weeping, and he, feeling the strong pity which is ever allied to a noble passion, satisfied or hopeless, swore to be patient with her, ay, and to serve and watch her tenderly from this day forward for evermore.

And she ? Only a low moan of " Archie !

Archie! my Darling; you said for Eternity,
did you regret your vow when Time was
nearly over? my Love! my only, only
Love!"

*   *   *   *   *   *

"Is not the gleaning of the grapes of
Ephraim better than the vintage of
Abiezer?"

CHAPTER X.

THE STORY OF YOUNG MAY MORN.

" O, it came o'er my ear like the sweet sound,
That breathes upon a bank of violets
Stealing and giving odour."

SHAKESPEARE.

IT was a great mortification to her mother that Ingha di Garcelli so stead-fastly maintained her decision of not marrying. She was now on the eve of possessing her accumulated inheritance,

and, as it would make her in every respect
independent of control, the Marchesa
dreaded that her maternal influence would
anon have less power in bringing about
any matrimonial scheme which she deemed
desirable.

Ingha's safeguard against the temptations
to frivolity, in which disappointment too
often seeks excitement, was the gratification she ever found in the pursuit of her
art. It was the magical golden thread
which still bound her to her lover; though
parted from him, and knowing almost
nothing of his present experiences, she
kept faith with herself, and so was true to
her ideal of life, believing that, so long as
they both laboured to attain the same

goal, they would one day have the reward they most desired.

She performed the duties that claimed her sweetly and seriously, and had no leisure to search for novelties nor for new sensations; her study of music and practice of her voice filled all the hours she could take from other engagements, and *ennui* from inertness or from lack of occupation she never experienced. Ingha's voice had become a marvel of exquisite power, and verily she had attained the wish of her earlier years; she had now the gift of song in a rare degree, but she never knew how great was her inspiration, and her unconsciousness of her genius was remarkable.

Marie did not spend the season in London as Ruy had expected. She came up to see her brother, but remained only a fortnight, and returned to her friends at Invean, having promised Ingha that she would stay with her all the following year.

Ingha knew of Ruy being established in Kensington, and, as the weeks went by, she, eagerly expectant, looked in every fresh scene, hoping for a glimpse of the form that was ever easily perceived amid a crowd of its fellows; but Ruy's haunts were not those frequented by the Garcellis, and so Ingha looked in vain.

Lady Kinaire, quick and observant, especially in matters which concerned the happiness of her friends, noticed that often when she met Ingha unexpectedly in the park, or elsewhere, she appeared to be looking for some one, and that her expression was then perturbed and anxious, and she noted also that the girl was ever ready to accede to any proposal to visit places where there were public gatherings; and Lady Kinaire conned these things over in her clever, little, Irish head.

Ingha never missed any opportunity of going to picture exhibitions, for there she naturally thought she would be more likely to meet Ruy than elsewhere: she might have met him over and over again at these places, for often she went the same days that he too chose, but Ingha's opportunities did not occur in the early mornings, and Ruy never went to them at other hours.

Lady Kinaire divined the cause of Ingha's disquiet, and determined to find out Mr. Montgomerie and, if possible, to discover what probability there still remained of her pet romance ending happily. She procured his address from Marie, and did not lose any time in devising an excuse for calling upon him.

Ruy received the visit with some surprise and much cordiality, for he had always felt a sincere liking for the bright, little lady who had, in the old days, been uniformly genial and friendly to him.

After their first greetings were over, Lady Kinaire said :

"We have so often missed you during all these long years, and now I suppose you are so much devoted to art you would consider time wasted on our interests and pleasures."

"No time could be wasted in your society," Ruy answered, "but my work is my main consideration, and I find it very exigent, as you doubtless know."

"They tell me," said Lady Kinaire, "that you paint portraits, and I am most anxious to have my child's. Will you accept the commission? I think you will not find him an ugly subject, and, as I will gladly myself bring Harold to you for the sittings, I will try to prevent him boring you very much."

Her tone was so winning, Ruy could not have refused even if he had wished, but, as he had a premonition that association with the Kinaires might bring him into contact with Ingha, he resolutely determined to check any social intercourse that was not connected with the work which alone could bring them ultimately together.

A little further conversation about the kind of portrait she wanted, half an hour spent in looking over the contents of Montgomerie's atelier, and Lady Kinaire departed.

The weeks wore on, Harold's picture proceeded, but, during the sittings, Lady Kinaire discovered that the artist became increasingly absorbed in his work. She would fain have spoken of Ingha, but opportunity never occurred, save for the mention of her name, when Ruy always maintained a studied silence.

Little Harold liked his visits to the atelier, and, after the second week, Lady Kinaire thought it better to leave the child and to call for him when the sitting was over.

Ruy had a very winning and sympathetic way with children, and they rarely wearied of his company. He had fascinated Harold by descriptions of the ad-

ventures of an imaginary traveller, and
the boy, who was as bright and clever as
his mother, appreciated the unusual character of Ruy's style of relating a story, for
it went on at each sitting, and Ruy always
left off when Harold seemed most interest-
ed in it, so that the child was eager
enough to return to him.

One day, when the two were alone, portrait and history alike proceeding, the one
to the satisfaction of the artist, the other
to the delight of the sitter, Harold interrupted Ruy's narrative by asking
abruptly:

"But did you ever see Young May Morn
again?"

"*I* see her, Harold? I am telling you a story about Eric the Wanderer, and the people *he* saw thousands of miles from here."

"I know that," answered Harold, as if he did not require the information, "but *you* are Eric, and Chum is Jarl, and you call yourself names to make a story. Miss di Garcelli thinks so."

"Miss di Garcelli!" said Ruy, looking at Harold. "Who told her?"

"Oh, I did. You know, she's a friend of mine, and when I go to see Kenneth she tells us stories, such nice ones, and sings songs in them. Kenneth doesn't understand all of them, but I do. I'm older and bigger than Kenneth, and Miss di Garcelli is first-rate. *You* would like her, I'm sure."

" Will you turn your face round a little, Harold ? You don't sit so still to-day."

"Don't I ? Well, I'll try, but tell me, Mr. Montgomerie, have you got a sweetheart ? I have, and she's so pretty, and dances with me at parties, and I'm going to marry her soon. Have *you* got a sweetheart, like Eric had ?"

" I never go to parties, Harold," said Ruy, smiling. " I have to work all

the time. I'm not so well off as
you."

"Well, I'll tell mother I want you at
my next party. Miss di Garcelli is coming,
and you'll see her, and I'm sure you
will say she is just as beautiful as Young
May Morn. May I look at that book
on the table?" added the boy, who did
not wait for an answer, but went to the
table where the coveted book was lying.

Ruy either did not remember that there
were several sketches in it, or did not
heed Harold's request, for the drawings
fluttered about the table before Ruy perceived what the child was doing.

"Oh, how pretty!" said the boy. "Who
is this?"

"Oh! these are only a few sketches of Young May Morn," answered Ruy, in some confusion, as he gathered them up again.

"They are just like Miss di Garcelli!" exclaimed Harold. "I told you she was quite as pretty as Young May Morn. I wish you would let me take these to show her."

"Why, Harold?"

"Because she asked me what Young May Morn was like, but I did not know, and I could only tell her that she used to sing in the canoe when Eric was away from her, and that always brought him back again."

"Well, and what did Miss di Garcelli say?" asked Ruy, with a wild longing for some token of her remembrance of the past.

"She said she wished *she* knew the pretty songs that Young May Morn could sing."

At this moment Lady Kinaire returned; she said, on entering:

"I am sure you must be tired of my boy; I did not mean to be so long in coming, but I was unexpectedly detained."

"I have been more than ever delighted," answered Ruy, with sincerity, putting aside the sketches of Young May Morn.

"I am only sorry the portrait will be so soon completed."

"Mother," said Harold, "Mr. Montgomerie has never been to a party, and he hasn't got a sweetheart yet; won't you ask him to come on my birthday?"

"Yes, Harold, and I intended to ask Mr. Montgomerie if he would come to Invereethin for the twelfth," said Lady Kinaire, winningly. "If you would visit us, we should be so very much pleased, and you should have plenty of opportunity to complete the picture, and to paint others too, if you wished. Will you be able to join us?"

"You are very kind," answered Ruy, "but I have already declined Mrs. Camp-

bell's invitation to Invean for the sake of
remaining at my work. I do most sincerely appreciate your kindness in asking
me, but I hope you will excuse me, for I
am compelled to deny myself."

"But, though Harold's picture be fin-
ished, I trust we shall not lose sight of
each other," said Lady Kinaire, kindly.

"I hope not," answered Ruy. "When
you come back to town, perhaps you will
find time to look in and see that I have not
been idle during your absence. You will
always be sure of a welcome, even if I have
no new pictures to show you."

And so they parted, and Lady Kinaire
acknowledged to herself that she had
effected nothing towards the object that

had prompted her to seek intercourse with Ruy Montgomerie.

Not yet, my lady.

CHAPTER XI.

GORE PROPOSES A BREAK IN HIS FRIEND'S
ASCETIC LIFE.

" But somewhere, unless love forget
His old way,
There shall be something better yet,
—Ay, some day."

O'SHAUGHNESSY.

A NOTHER autumn glided by; the
heather bloomed again at Kerinvean, though unseen and untrodden by
him who yearned for the fresh breezes

that wafted its incense across the land.

Inexorable and uncompromising toil had taken the place of the long, tireless tramps over moor and hill; the salmon swam the waters scathless for him who had once been so merciless in his raids upon them, and stag and grouse alike were free from his unerring aim. But his thoughts were not bounded by the walls of the atelier where he laboured, and sometimes, when a bitter wave of memory broke on the barren shore of his monotonous Present, an utterable longing took possession of him, the overwhelming desire that comes to all who have to struggle on alien ground, the uncontrollable, quenchless thirst that can be slacked by no near

flow, and, alas! the mighty ones, they,
too, are far, and no one bringeth the
coveted " water of the well of Bethlehem
that is at the gate !"

An after gloom, too, assailed Ruy with its
dreary, hopeless, endless prospect of working on and on alone, in the years to come.
He might perchance one day compel fame,
if so be that Fate willed it, but how to
bring love into his life he could not foresee. His comparative poverty always
rose up between him and a bright, possible future, and Kerinvean's words, " her
immense fortune," were ever ready to
recur to his mind ; and with no one to
suggest hope, no one to give the praise
which sympathy ever prompts at the need-

ed moment, what wonder that his courage sometimes almost failed?

Yet the name of Roderiguc Montgom-erie was becoming known. The sums he received for his pictures—alas! his dreams of marble were none of them yet realized —were fair and satisfactory, but he could not be persuaded to exhibit save in his own studio.

Some of his artist acquaintances envied his "luck" in being able to get along without yielding to custom, others laughed at him for eccentricity, and the public naturally put its own con-struction on this abstinence, which was, as usual with the public, a construction wide of the mark.

Ruy had kept some of his theories in-
violate through the hardships of his experience, and one of these was, that art
has other ends than the mere acquisition
of a livelihood, and he shrank from the
" big shops," where the pell-mell, mis-
placed crowding of works of fancy and
but rarely of imagination, made the brain
whirl, and the heart sick with surfeit.
His visit to the galleries did not resemble
the ordinary scrambling through them ;
he went sometimes to look at one picture
only, and would unobtrusively stay by it
till its beauty had penetrated all his
soul, and then he would come away, hardly glancing at any other : this was his
instinctively courteous tribute to great

endeavour. It might be said that a man would not have time to effect much work who had to make a separate visit for the study of each picture in the annual exhibitions. Certainly not, but Montgomerie had no desire (and why should he?) to examine all the wonders there available, and I trow he had the best of it, in eschewing the majority.

And he carried out his theory regarding his own completed works; so long as they remained in his possession each was shown by itself, with no distractions, nothing by its side to amuse nor sadden, just the one picture alone to impress the looker on. It was not that he had fear of competing, for he always ranked his skill on the lowest step of the ladder of art, and it was his constant merciless comparison of his own work with that which he considered masterly, that often depressed him and prostrated his hope.

Notwithstanding that his elected mode of making known his work was one that is ever slow and hard, he had his followers, men who appreciated genius, though it was claimed by no particular society, and his pictures were bought by these heterodox patrons who were audacious enough to spend their money on that which to them was "bread," instead of moving earth and sky to procure "a stone."

There are still those who judge the

merits of art work without the aid of the
managers of the markets of this generation, though those who bow the knee to
Baal are a vast majority, composed of the
brotherhood of fashion in art, critics, and
dealers, who all, by turn, pronounce their
incontrovertible *ipse dixit* of " genuine !" or
" inimitable !" or " marvellous !" upon that
which has neither beauty nor suggestion of
peace to him who yearns for both. Happy
is the lover of Nature aspiring to the knowledge of art who is not scared when he
hears the customary wrangling over these
so-called masterpieces, for, alas! the jar-
gon concerning them is alike confusing and
incessant ; and yet where is he who dare

aver that the day may not come when he
too shall ally himself with those who
shout "Bene!" when the cry should be a
loud and universal "Miserere!"

Autumn and winter waned, the Kerinvean household came early back to town,
and Marie was of the party.

Ingha had now absolute control of her
fortune, and lavish she was in the use of
it, more especially when she could aid the
needy, and she never lost an opportunity
of helping or encouraging artists; they
were the principal poor of her world, and
she regarded this mission to be rare and
unequivocal, which she had no choice but
to fulfil, and very devotedly she set about

M 2

her duty. She understood but little of business, but, with Marie to assist her, she determined to put aside no claim that came from those who laboured in art.

She insisted on defraying all expenses incurred by Kerinvean on her account, and had several servants and horses for her own use. She tried by every possible means to make Marie benefit by the change, and shared all her pleasures with her friend; her own personal gratification she rarely considered, and was always ready to give of her abundance where need was known to her.

When the girls drove out together Marie never asked Ingha to turn her

ponies in the direction of Ruy's house ;
though she herself spent hours with him,
he maintained such a significant silence
about her daily associates, Marie felt too
much perplexed to try to bring them together. Eager as Ingha was watching for
a chance meeting with Ruy, it had not yet
occurred.

In the earlier London seasons the
Marchesa had exercised a baffling ingenuity in monopolising the time Marie and
Ingha would fain have spent in different
pursuits, but Marie's retirement had put
an end to engagements being arranged for
her, and Ingha's independent position now
induced her mother to allow her more
freedom in the choice of her occupations.

Kerinvean chafed to find his presence so often required by his wife in fulfilling her social obligations. Town life was always irksome to him, and had it not been for his devotion to his son he would have spent more time in Scotland, but the Marchesa had decreed that London suited the boy, so the fond father acquiesced with a good grace.

Early in the season Lady Kinaire had planned a great amateur musical perform-ance for the benefit of a charity in which her interest had been excited, and she had determined that this, the only entertain-ment of the kind she had ever given, should be an undoubted success, and she

knew it could only be effected by obtaining Ingha's co-operation.

Ingha entered into the scheme with her
wonted enthusiasm, readily promising to
give all the aid in her power, and, as Lady
Kinaire had also secured the most skilful
amateur force in town, the arrangements
were soon completed.   The Kinaires knew
how to plan a brilliant entertainment, and
neither trouble nor ingenuity was spared.
A large hall was hired, and exquisitely
decorated, and ante-rooms were arranged
for the performers and also for the audience.

On the afternoon of the night of the concert Ingha was driving Marie, when Fate

decreed that Ruy should be walking in the same neighbourhood, and that they should meet him; the ponies went swiftly by, for Ingha had not perceived him till it was too late for recognition; it was Marie nodding silently to her brother that attracted her, and for a few moments she said not a word, but her hands trembled as with strong repression she tried to keep back the tears from the eyes that had so long and vainly sought what they had just missed.

Gentle reader! would you have been more stoical? Would you have behaved one degree better? You might probably have used an elegant expletive to express your feelings, but I think that, if for five years you had been waiting for some great desire—though only the glimpse of a dear, denied face—when it crossed your path unaware, you would not have borne the chagrin more bravely than she of whom I write.

" Marie, the wind is cold," she only said; " shall we drive straight home ?"

" After a meteor has flashed across a darkened sky, the gloom is tenfold greater than when we watched for the chance falling of a star !" was Ruy's thought as he sped back to his lonely rooms.

He knew by the rushing blood and thrilling nerves that it was her lovely face he had seen at his sister's side. Unstrung and miserable he sat down in his vacant room to think and ponder over the brief glimpse that had had so strange an effect upon him.

Presently the familiar sound of Dallas Gore's step fell on his ear, and the door opened, when the friends greeted each other warmly.

" Why, Montgomerie, you look as if you had seen a ghost; you've been working far too hard lately. I came in this afternoon to ask you to dine with me to-night. There's a rumour of war, and, while there's a chance of it, I'm on the alert, and shall feel unsettled till I know. Will you dine with me and go and hear some music afterwards ?"

"What music?" asked Ruy, abruptly, at that moment feeling as if he did not care ever to hear another note in his life.

"Oh! it's Lady Kinaire's concert, and I promised to go and take a lot of fellows. I've got a host of tickets disposed of, but I'm not going with Tom, Dick, and Harry. I was at Kinaire's at luncheon to-day and heard all the news. At the last moment the man who has been practising with Miss di Garcelli has had to leave town, and she, in despair, has got your sister to take this fellow's place, she being the only one who is accustomed to play her accompaniments."

"Marie going to perform in public!" said Ruy, amazed.

"Yes; isn't it good of her to put her own inclinations aside to prevent the concert becoming a failure? I wish you would go with me; she would be far less nervous if you were present."

"Nervous. Who?" asked Ruy, quickly, stooping to stroke Chum who had listened intently to the whole conversation. "Must I go, Chummie?" he added in an undertone, whereupon Chum wagged his tail and pushed his black, cold nose against Ruy approvingly.

"Marie—your sister, I mean," returned Gore, "has been so long unaccustomed to this sort of thing. They say several of the profession have been trying to get tickets, there is such a *furore* about Miss di Garcelli's voice; besides, she's so awfully handsome, and such a favourite. You haven't seen her lately?" added Gore, questioningly.

"Yes, I saw her to-day," answered Ruy, gravely. " I will go with you. Where do we dine ?"

" At my club at seven o'clock. The concert begins at nine ; I promised Kinaire to be there early."

Sir Dallas hurried away lest Ruy should repent his decision ; he had never dreamed of obtaining his consent; but Ruy had tasted the sweet sorrow of a mere glimpse of her whom his tired soul yearned for continually; his parched lips had been near the fountain which alone could refresh him, and still his thirst was not quenched.

CHAPTER XII.

"THE KING IS WANTING MEN, MY DEAR!"

HALF-PAST nine o'clock. The hall was filled with a brilliant assemblage, and the concert had just begun.

Ingha di Garcelli was strangely excited, and even when Lord Kinaire led her forward for her first song, she had not overcome the depression consequent on her disappointment during the drive.

Sir Dallas arrived in time to accompany

Marie to the pianoforte : there was quite a
sensation amongst the audience as the two
lovely performers appeared ; both were
dressed in white. Marie's attire was very
simple, but exquisitely suited to her graceful figure, soft lace about her throat and
arms, Archie's glittering stone her only
jewel. Ingha's gleaming pearls and white
roses enhanced the glorious beauty that
was more than ever radiant to-night.

Sir Dallas had already told Marie that
her brother was among the audience, but
she had had no opportunity of letting
Ingha know, for they had been surrounded
by people till the moment they had to
appear ; Marie trusted to Fate that her
friend would not be taken by surprise dis-

covering Ruy's presence suddenly, but the eyes that have long been watching grow very keen, and the heart that has long been waiting is alway bewildered by the verity of its own hope.

Ere the first tone of her voice reached Ruy, he had to rise to give room to a lady to pass to a seat beyond his, and for a few seconds Ingha's friends thought she would have broken down ; her voice trembled through the few bars of a difficult recitative, and "stage fright," as her tremor was called, fought hard for mastery, but the recitative was over at last, and Ingha knew she would either fail miserably or sing as she had never sung before, so her pride came to her aid, though little would

have made those unshed tears of the
afternoon fall in torrents on her
roses.

She gathered her courage to repress her
emotion, dreading failure before him of
whom alone she thought, and when the
soft strains of the aria, on which Marie,
perceiving Ingha's perturbation, dwelt
lingeringly, stole over her spirit, she gave
herself up to her work, held her roses
tight, and no one would have dreamed of
her heart throbs when her voice took
wing; she let it soar in its own sweet ring-
ing clearness out into the world of doubt
and desire. There was no trembling of
purpose apparent, nor a shadow of failure;

but her face was pale, and her eyes bright
and eager.

" Bravo! bravo!" said again and again
the delighted audience, and she bowed her
acknowledgment of their applause, but
gave not one glance to the place where,
far behind the front rows, Ruy sat spell-
bound and enthralled.

In the ante-room Ingha was warmly
congratulated.

" I have heard that stage fright is a
phase amateurs never quite overcome,"
said Sir Dallas, kindly; " but you did sing
gloriously towards the end."

" It wasn't stage fright," answered
Ingha; " I think I lost my way, and the

people all seemed to be laughing at me, but I will behave better in my next song."

The concert proceeded with great spirit, but it is no part of our story to describe the performance, save the portion in which Ingha di Garcelli displayed her wondrous gift. Ruy was quite insensible to other influences; he waited for her, and, when she again appeared, he drank in the sweetness of the vision, and listened with all his soul to the luring melody of her tones.

When she came for the last time she was serenely composed, and her peaceful face betokened no recognition nor memory of the past. Her song was a little ballad

of the day, with a minor refrain of hopeless love, a wail for the joy of bygone
years, and she crooned it so pathetically
that it went straight to the hearts of those
fine people who listened, for fine people have
hearts, and many a pang of tender sorrow
is felt under *point de gaze* and diamonds,
notwithstanding we often hear quite the
contrary.

Ingha smiled and bowed as the applause
became deafening, but her yearning had
spent itself in the sorrow of her song, and
now she hoped to escape from the crowd
and weep the tears she owed her own
despair. But the fine people were determined to hear her again, it was not every
night they had the chance of treating one

of themselves to the test of the enthusiastic begging for over and above the bargain to which they subject the profession, and they made the most of the present opportunity; besides, Miss di Garcelli was so munificent in her givings, a song more or less would be nothing to her.

"Kinaire," said old General Gordon, "ask her for a Scotch song."

Lord Kinaire repeated the request while Ingha stood reluctant, and the applause and cheering grew louder and louder.

"Marie, can you recall 'The king is wanting men, my dear'?"

"Oh, yes: will you sing it?"

"I will try," answered Ingha.

"All of it?" asked Marie, in a lower tone. "Your verse too?"

"Yes, especially my verse," said the girl, with strangely quiet decision in her tone.

And then came the triumph of the night; but Ingha was not thinking of triumph, only of a bend in the river at Kerinvean in an autumn evening far away in the past, and of a voice that pleaded for a song ere the myriad stars shone forth. And she, standing there before the crowd in her superb womanhood, in silken sheen, with the perfume of the white roses wafting around her, recalling in vivid bitterness his gifts long years ago, sang the same song to him again, adding a wail that Life's dreary experience had inspired.

The audience listened intently to every word, but he, her lover, knew she was singing alone for him.

> "Oh! the king is wanting men, my dear,
>   And I for one must go,
>   And for the very life of me
>   I darna answer no!
>   For I am bound to go, my love,
>   Where no one shall me know,
>   But the bonny lassie's answer
>   Was aye, no, no!
>
> "Oh! I'll cut off my yellow hair,
>   And go along with thee,

And I'll be thy faithful comrade
In a foreign countree.
For I am bound to go, my love,
Where no one shall me know,
But the bonny lassie's answer
Was aye, no, no !

" Oh, stay at home, my dearest dear,
And dinna gang wi' me,
For it's little, little do ye ken
The dangers of the sea.
For I am bound to go, my love,
Where no one shall me know,
But the bonny lassie's answer
Was aye, no, no !"

The laddie sailed sae far awa'
Beyond her ken at hame.
She waited, waited faithfully,
But ah ! he never came.

And hearts forlorn are bound to break,

For love is full of woe:

But wad she tak her fond vow back?

I trow, no, no!

The applause was loud and prolonged, bouquets were thrown at Ingha's feet, and among them a wreath of white roses, which Lord Kinaire gave to her. She seemed in a trance, and all suddenly her gaze went over the crowd in search of Ruy, and for one brief, wild moment the rush of memories in both hearts was unutterable.

The Marchesa, regarding her daughter, proud of her rare beauty, as well as of her splendid success, said to the ever sympathetic little Kathleen Kinaire, who,

like her friend, did not dream of Ruy's
presence :

"Ingha is wonderfully composed considering."

CHAPTER XIII.

SAINT CECILIA.

"All the great men *see* what they paint before they paint it,—see it in a perfectly passive manner,—cannot help seeing it if they would ; whether in their mind's eye, or in bodily fact, does not matter ; . . . . it being to them in its own kind and degree always a true vision or Apocalypse, and invariably accompanied in their hearts by a feeling correspondent to the words, ' Write the things *which thou hast seen, and* the things which *are.*' "

RUSKIN.

AND Ruy?

The uncoutrollable impulse that

had prompted him to accompany Sir Dallas to the concert had kept him listening as in a dream, though Ingha's presence was not one whit more real to him than it had been through all the dreary years of his lonely struggling, in which there would have been no gleams of hope save for her, and, intangible as they had been, they had shed a lingering light on the mazes of his effort and labour.

As her voice thrilled his soul with its ecstatic sweetness, and the familiar strains wandered like a rare bird's song in the world of his dreams, Ruy sat in a transport of exquisite feeling, unconscious of all other influences. The rapture which

her singing was wont to give him was unspeakably intensified to-night; she cast
the unforgotten sweet spells upon him;
even the first trembling echoes of the recitative had the same compelling power as
of old, which he remembered so well to-
night.

Anon, when Ingha's strong will had
repressed all her disquiet, the stream of
melody flowed on; it seemed to Ruy that
the sluice-gates were opened, and his dry,
arid thirst recklessly drank in the refresh-
ing flood, as only they can quaff who have
been long athirst in sight of rivers remote
and inaccessible.

Montgomerie's intent face was still and

calm, it gave no indication of his rapturous
emotion ; he seemed to know no one, nor to
care for none, for all suddenly the current
of his life had reached the infinite sea;
there were no longer any hindrances to his
course, the great waves of joy rolled on,
and their white glistening crests told of
triumphant gladness ; he was a struggling
artist no more, but rather, for the hour,
one inspired, to whom the glorious visions
of his boyhood came back with the dew
of youth and hope upon them. As the
night wore on his love waxed bold, he
seemed at last to be grasping the star
that had lighted the gloom of his night,
and he knew full well that her serene

orbit had not been disturbed by the crossing of any other whose magnitude had eclipsed his own in her faithful reckoning.

At length Ingha's allotted part of the programme having been sung, the encore was vociferously demanded, and he, who had never once applauded, waited with an impetuous desire, in which fear was mingled; he yearned that some act of hers would link the past with to-day, that present bliss might for a brief moment shut out the years of drear misery that had separated them. Oh! for one halcyon near glimpse of his Elysium, ere Fate again drove him from its shores to the dark and lonely waters, whose winds

might never more bring him within sight
of the Isles of the Blessed, of which the
beauty and promise were now delighting
his soul.

He waited breathlessly till she began
the tender little ballad that had so pro-
phetically touched him when she had sung
it at the river-side for him alone. But
the last verse was new to him, and, as the
words came forth in those tenderly pathetic strains that are only ever possible
to a violin or to a human voice, a wild
irrepressible joy, for all the song's pathos,
took possession of Ruy; he knew that
Ingha had composed the sequel to the
ballad, and why?

The applause was renewed, and, as Ingha

bowed again and again to the audience, it
seemed to her that the noise would never
cease, and it was then for the second time
that night that her longing eyes met
Ruy's.

He was standing when her gaze for a
transient recognition sought his; her impulse to see him once more was no less
overwhelming than Montgomerie's yearning for the look she gave, and in that
blissful greeting her beauty seemed to
him incomparably beyond his memory of
it, wholly transfigured as it was by the
intensity of her love, and the excitement of an experience, sorrowful as it
was sweet.

Out into the night went Ruy, impelled by a wish to transfer the vision he had seen into art; for, alas! by no other way could he be brought to his goal. Should he succeed, she at least would be obeyed, for had she not years ago told him to paint Saint Cecilia, and had not the time now come when he felt possessed of the power to accomplish ? Full of her inspiration, he quickly sped through the streets, and it seemed to him that the lights thereof were all stars singing in their courses, and that the bitter east wind bore to him the perfume of thousands of whitest roses from the blooming gardens of the Hesperides.

On reaching his home he did not sit down to brood over the events of the night, did not purposelessly live over and over again the sweet moments of enthralment. A subtle power forced him to act, and, telling Chum he was going to work, Chum acquiesced, and went back to his corner, from whence he came at nights, for his most cherished pleasure, which consisted in listening to Ruy's stories of the future. In these his master always prophesied happy hunting grounds for him, like Kerinveau, where Chum should have his soul no longer vexed with the obsequious addresses of curs, nor the purring of cats with claws, nor with mice whose fleetness too often eluded his grip.

Chum never insisted on his own amuse-
ment, and, if Ruy were not in the mood for
story-telling, the wise Eskimo always
waited till another opportunity; he and
his master both possessed the disappoint-
ment-bearing courage that makes spirits
patient.

Ruy went straightway to his atelier, put
a bare canvas on an easel, and ere he
went to rest had sketched upon it the face
and form of her who was the love of his
whole life, as she had appeared when her
yearning gaze, rapturous and sorrowful,
had sought his, when her very hands had
seemed about to stretch over the crowd to
stay his going.

Her own conception of Saint Cecilia at

last, and, though Ruy had sought that look
of mingled joy, love, and grief in faces
wherever he had wandered, never had he
seen it till now. There was in it the
infinite yearning that comes into human
eyes but rarely, which Ingha had described
as her idea of Cecilia's emotion when
Valerian was inspired with courage to
fulfil a martyrdom cruel as his love was
strong.

The picture was faithfully designed,
even to the wreath, of which the "Sanc-
torale Catholicum" makes full mention
in its short account of this most sublime
of all the saints, of whom, alas! we
know so little, even the organ of the

" Confraternity of the Sacred Christ, and
Agony of our Lord," containing but four
pages about Saint Cecilia. How remarkable it is that all the traditions of the
Romish church are both brief and
confused. The scant records of her
noblest martyrs are ever made sub-
servient to the supernatural, and her
gravest historians mislead us as to the
undoubtedly marvellous gifts of those
of whom they write. The chronicles,
alike of saint and sinner, are a tangled
web of mystical lore, from which it
is ever difficult to unravel the suppressed thread of the real life and
work.

Ruy felt that this picture would decide whether his power in art was God-given or mere acquirement, and he toiled unremittingly upon it, essaying nothing meanwhile, save the same subject in clay. He worked for weeks with the old Titanic force which he had ever at will when the dominant idea was stronger than the ordinary every day inducement, and his energy was as unwearying as when Archie and he together tried in the early days to force their luck.

"What have we here?" asked a rich dealer who frequented Ruy's studio, and sometimes bespoke his pictures before they had left the easel, and who had been to-day announced in the atelier ere. Ruy had had time to screen his work.

"Oh, nothing but a design so far, but I hope it will develope into St. Cecilia by-and-by," answered Ruy, wishing this visitor had not seen the canvas.

"You have got a rare model," persisted the dealer, "but the subject is a mistake; it's worn out and threadbare. Society at present cares nothing for saints and martyrs, and would rather not be reminded of their having ever existed."

"But we don't paint altogether for the present," said Ruy, "and the face I am working on does not suggest a picture I shall offer for sale."

"But you *will* sell it, notwithstanding," remarked the dealer, decisively. "The most eccentric of you would far sooner see the best thing he ever did on another man's wall than on his own; it's the natural love of appreciation with which some of us are gifted more than others. I like this face. I wish you would use it for a popular theme, and give up your idea of canonizing your model."

Ruy smiled, and tried to change the subject, but the dealer was an obstinate specimen of the class, and possessed an impregnable belief in his own unassailable tenets of art, as well as in his own really circumscribed knowledge of character.

" There isn't the least approval amongst the *connoisseurs* for ideal religious subjects," said he. " Goddesses and syrens, smiling or weeping, nude or no, it matters not, have far more chance; and a beautiful face, however cleverly painted, is handicapped for the buying public if you essay to make a saint of her. The ignorant, who are the majority, don't know who she was, and don't want to know, and so the idea you aim at is often quite obscured to them. But with the other subjects the idea is nearly always apparent, and meets a quick response."

"But the best work has rarely met anything but slow appreciation," ventured Montgomerie.

"Truly; but why not paint for your contemporaries? It's just as philanthropic, and a good deal more remunerative, than working for a generation unborn that can never give you any sort of return."

Ruy smiled as he shook his head incredulously.

"Will you give up your idea of saintship, and paint this face as a popular theme?" asked the dealer.

"We will talk of something else," said Ruy, quite content with silence till his picture should speak its own defence.

Did ever any man, knowing he had work to do the impulse to which was inexorable and absolute, did ever such accomplish, nay even fairly commence that work, without being warned that some other duty was much better suited to the times and to his powers, and that this, which revealed itself imperatively to him was a mere illusion, and would never reach the acme of the ignorant—success? Cruellest of fate is that in which the toiler never can discern the possibility of any divine accomplishment, and it is ever wiser to let the failure, fore-

seen of him who strives not, come in
the pursuit wherein the urgent bent
decrees.

CHAPTER XIV.

LADY KINAIRE ASSUMES THE RÔLE OF ART CRITIC.

"Do you not know I am a woman? When I
think, I must speak. Sweet; say on."

SHAKESPEARE.

A BITTER east wind was blowing on the
evening of the concert, and a sudden
chill made Ingha shiver as she went from
the hall to her carriage; that night
she could not sleep, and next day, tired,
but still somewhat excited, she asked

Marie to accompany her on a long drive.

The wind was still strong from the east, and, when Ingha returned home, she complained of hoarseness and unusual fatigue. The following day she became ill, and the doctor pronounced her suffering from a slight attack of inflammation of the lungs; the danger was soon over, and, when convalescent, she was advised to go to the south of France, or to try her native air, and singing was strictly forbidden.

Hardly had the physician left the house ere Ingha, dreading that her illness might have hurt her voice, opened the pianoforte of her boudoir, and, for the first time since the concert, played a few bars and essayed

to sing, but the sound that came was un-
familiar and strange ; she tried again, but
her will had no effect upon her vocal
organ ; weak and almost despairing, she
sank down on a couch and covered her
face, and Marie found her weeping bitterly.

"What is it, darling?" asked Marie,
kneeling beside her. "You seemed so
much better when I left you a few
minutes ago."

"I am better, Marie, quite well again,
but my voice has gone, and the doctor
knew it, and that was his reason for for-
bidding me even to attempt to sing,"
moaned the poor girl.

"But it will come back, sweetheart,

when you are strong; it is merely the effect of your illness, and you are sure to be able to sing again soon," said Marie, cheerfully.

"No, I cannot believe that, for on the concert night, when I had sung better than ever in my life, I felt, oh! so utterly desolate, as if I were losing what I prized more than anything that I possessed."

"But, Ingha dear, it was not your voice, I feel sure; it was only the effect of the excitement which you suppressed so well before the crowd."

"I could have borne any other loss," went on Ingha, mournfully; "so long as I had my art, I had pity to spare for care and pain, but now the most ignorant soprano in London is more to be envied than I with all my acquirements; she has hope and I have none."

Ingha would not be comforted, and the consequent depression retarded her recovery, so that several weeks passed ere she was able to go beyond her boudoir. Kerinvean and the Marchesa had been obliged to leave town with their delicate son, while Marie and Coyla gladly took the responsibility of the care of Ingha till the doctor should consider her able to join her mother abroad. But two months passed and still she stayed in London. June arrived, and news came that the rest of the household was to return soon from

France, and arrangements were being made for the whole party to go to Scotland. Marie and Ingha had heard of the departure of nearly all their friends from town, though Lady Kinaire remained. Sir Dallas Gore had left with his regiment for Zululand some time before.

Ingha's health was variable; the dejection that had settled on her spirit had short intervals of feverish zeal in which she pursued every plan suggested for regaining strength in the hope of her vocal power returning. Her physician assured her that time would effect the desired change; but she had been unaccustomed to life without her art, and everything else now seemed impotent to gratify her; the practice of it too was lacking, and it had ever yielded her unfailing delight, and had held an even balance in the mind that was now crushed on all sides with disappointment. Her art had been her shield against all ills till now; loss and grief could assail her only through it. So long as she could labour in it she had followed her ideal faithfully, had never swerved in her love and patient service, for the inward voice which had guided Saint Cecilia also had whispered to Ingha : "Be silent and wait!" The days passed in vacant hopelessness, complete re-covery seemed as far off as in the first hour when she discovered her voice was gone, and, with the loss of her occupation and delight, a growing impression settled upon her that the love and homage of her heart were dreams which she alone had cherished, and which now could never be fulfilled.

Lady Kinaire came often to see her two favourites, and much she grieved to note the fragile look daily increasing on Iugha's face, and was greatly perplexed to find a remedy.

One morning Iugha sent suddenly for her lawyer, and was engaged with him when Lady Kinaire arrived, and Marie informed her how their friend was occupied.

"I think," she added, "she is not quite so well to-day; she seems excited

and flushed, and is far more eager about
business than ever I saw her before."

"What business is pressing just now?"
asked Lady Kinaire.

"I do not know; she told me last
week her affairs were going on splendidly, that her investments for the or-
phans of artists and those for her
proposed school of music were doing
better than any other, and that she
thought she would soon be able to carry
out a project she was developing, to result
in a fund to enable poor art-students to
travel; but I conclude that it is quite a
fresh idea that has made her so anxious
to-day."

"How Quixotic she is!" said Lady

Kinaire; "but her plans, though romantic, are all so generous and practic-
able. When do you think she will go to
Kerinvean ?"

"Immediately after the return of the
others, if she be able; but she appears
as averse as ever to leave town."

Lady Kinaire made no answer, and
presently a message was brought asking
Marie and her friend to go to Ingha's
boudoir, where they found the invalid
lying on a couch evidently quite ex-
hausted, but with a strange, excited
expression in the eyes which regarded
them questioningly.

"What have you two been saying about
me? Don't be doleful. I am tired, but

it is the stupid business that has made me so. After to-morrow, I shall have peace. Where have you been this morning, Lady Kinaire? You look as bright and fresh as a dewdrop."

"I haven't been among the flowers to-day," answered Lady Kinaire, somewhat hesitatingly, "and yet I saw some painted white roses almost as lovely as your extravagant clusters. How many hundreds do you use in a week, Ingha?"

"I never count my benefits, only my cares and worries," said Ingha, smiling. "But where have you been, dear? I am sure you have had a nice experience. You look so radiant and glad."

"Really you are growing quite a flatterer, Ingha. I have only been to Mr. Montgomerie's rooms. Kinaire becomes more and more pleased with Harold's portrait, and he wanted me to ask your brother, Marie, if he would paint mine. His servant, unfortunately, showed me into the room where he was working at a picture evidently not meant to be seen, but, having seen it, I have come here to scold *you*, Ingha."

Ingha was listening hungrily to every word, but she showed a quiet face as she asked, in a repressed voice:

"For what are you going to scold me?"

"For not telling me you were giving

Mr. Montgomerie sittings," said Lady Kinaire. " I never saw anything more lovely
than your portrait; so appropriately called
' The vision of Saint Cecilia.' Perhaps
the life-like expression is more true than
the accuracy of the features, though it
is a very rare expression even with you.
Have you seen the picture yet ?"

"No," answered Ingha, and slowly and
quietly added the words, " I have not seen
it yet."

" The face is full of pathetic ecstacy.
I think, my dear," and Lady Kinaire
took Ingha's hand while speaking, "that
picture will widen the fame of your
beauty, while increasing the renown of
the artist; but I really don't know what

he will say, if you tell him I have given you a private criticism."

"I do not think we shall tell him," returned Ingha, with a slight tinge of bitterness in her tones.

"Now, my dears, I must go," said Lady Kinaire, rising. "I had only five minutes to give you, and I have stayed half an hour, but I will come again soon."

She had hardly glanced at Ingha, though she would fain have observed narrowly the effect of her recital. There was little difference apparent in Ingha's expression, and Lady Kinaire hurried away, somewhat nervous as to the result of her errand, but she trusted that love would overcome at last, and that the two who she had ever averred were predestined to bless each other would, ere too late, complete her cherished romance.

The day following was a rarely beautiful one, clear, warm, and bright; during the morning Ingha was again occupied with her lawyer, and, after his departure, Mistress Gilroy went about looking wistful and anxious. When the doctor came she told him the invalid was not so well, but he merely enjoined quiet, and, if possible, a drive to dissipate the symptoms of which Coyla had spoken.

Towards afternoon Ingha said to Marie timidly :

"You heard what the doctor said about

my going out? Will you drive my ponies to-day? I want to make an expedition."

" Of course, dear, I will drive you anywhere. What time will be best?" answered Marie, eagerly, pleased that Ingha should herself have proposed going out.

"Now remember, Marie, when I direct you this afternoon, you have given me a voluntary promise, because I am determined upon this visit, and I would prefer going with you."

"Where? You may tell me now. I won't go back on my word, dear," asked Marie, mystified about the project.

"I am going to your brother's studio,

Marie. I want to see this vision of Saint Cecilia. I have been waiting all my life to see it, and," Ingha added, wearily, " I am glad it is completed in time."

"But consider, Ingha, Kerinvean and the Marchesa will——"

"Yes, I know they will," interrupted Ingha, "unutterable things, Marie! but you don't mind, do you, sweetheart? And, though I have conjured up the very worst, I find it hasn't the least weight with my determination."

Marie's strong sympathy was awakened, and she remonstrated no more.

Ingha's eyes were bright and her face flushed, as she leaned back in her phaeton and spoke to Marie.

"Now, darling," she said, "I have planned everything.   I want you to go first to
him, and tell him I will follow soon, and
if he refuse to receive me,"—here her
voice trembled—"ask him to let me spend
an hour with his picture ; but, listen, I
want to be alone with it, a whole short
hour, Marie !"

And to Marie recurred the words,
"And I, I want you for a whole long
Eternity !" and the scene where they were
uttered in some indefinable way mingled
with the emotion of the present hour, and
she answered, quickly :

"My darling, I will do anything you
wish ; you are so dear to me."

"Marie, if you make love to me, I

shall break down, and," she added, in a gayer tone, " this afternoon I mean to be a Spartan !"

CHAPTER XV.

A SPARTAN.

> " Then she held forthe her lily-white hand
>   Towards that knight so free ;
> He gave to it one gentill kisse,
> His heart was brought from bale to blisse,
>   The tears sterte from his ee."
>
> CHAUCER.

THE ponies were soon drawn up at Ruy's door. Finding that her brother was at home, Marie descended, and with trembling fingers Ingha took the reins and drove off, intending to return shortly, as arranged.

Marie went straight to Ruy's atelier, where she announced herself, but he came to her quickly before she could advance to the easel on which his work was placed.

" How are you, Ruy ?" said Marie. "Ingha drove me here."

"Did she?" answered her brother, a flush mantling his face and brow. "Is your friend better? You look pale yourself, Marie ; you are not ill, dear ?"

"Oh! I am quite well, Ruy ; but I think Ingha seems worse, and she has taken an odd notion about coming here to see your picture."

"Here! which picture? I don't understand you, Marie."

His sister told him the burden of Lady
Kinaire's conversation the day before, and
timidly ended by saying:

"You will receive Ingha, won't you,
Ruy?"

"Certainly," said her brother, a wild
joy thrilling his spirit; "when will she
come?"

"To-day, in a few minutes; but, before she arrives, will you permit me to
look at your Saint Cecilia?"

Ruy went round to the front of his
easel, and, beckoning Marie to follow, he
said, gravely:

"I fear you may be as dissatisfied

with it as I myself sometimes feel."

Marie was deeply moved by the marvellous beauty of the likeness, but she could not gaze as long as she wished, for soon she heard the ponies stop again at the door, and, as Ruy left her to go and meet Ingha, she hurried to another room, where she gladly waited an anxious but hopeful hour.

Ingha was slowly ascending the steps as Ruy went forward. She held out her hand, but words for the moment were difficult to both.

" Will you come at once to my atelier?" asked Ruy, not tempted to make any vacant conventional compliments about the honour of the visit.

And she only answered a low " Yes " as he led the way.

On entering the studio, Chum bounded forward and sniffed at Ingha's dress, and she, bending down, said :

" Do you know me, Chum ?"

Chum did not answer save by a greeting, the like of which he had never accorded to anyone but to Sir Dallas Gore at Pniel. He licked her hands and breathed hard with excitement, and, when Ingha sat down, he tried to keep her attention by many manifestations of dumb, demonstrative delight; he nestled his head in the folds of her gown, and looked up into her face with an unspeakable affection that conveyed his unutterable gladness. Then he went to Ruy's side in an apologetic manner, as if he too ought to be made a partaker in the rejoicing, and Chum wagged his handsome tail as he walked between Ingha and his master with an air as one who would say, " I told you so ; I knew we should find her again !"

After Ingha had been in the room a few seconds, although she tried to re-press her cough, the exertion she had un-dergone brought it back. Ruy perceived how frail she was, and that the few weeks of illness had greatly changed her appear-ance. Her pallor was modified by a slight flush on her cheeks, but her eyes were unnaturally eager and bright. She was dressed in white, and she held a perfect rose in her hand.

"I am so sorry," she said, "to entertain you with this, but I am unfortunate in not being able to prevent it."

"I did not think you were so ill," said Montgomerie, gently, forcing back the impulse that prompted more passionate pity, for he saw the effect of the excitement and slight fatigue she had encountered were almost too much for her strength.

"I am not ill, not very ill," she answered, somewhat bitterly; "anyone may have a cough, that is nothing."

"But yours is painful," Ruy said, meeting her timid glance by a grave and tender expression of countenance.

"Surely, after five years of separation, we have other things to speak of than the symptoms of an illness. I hope you forgive me for coming here unbidden. I think you know—if you have not forgotten—that it has been the wish of my life to see a faithful picture of Saint Cecilia, and yours is sure to be beautiful."

"I have not forgotten one word of all the few you ever uttered to me," said Montgomerie, somewhat sternly; "the happiest moments of my life have been ever impossible to forget. You laid your commands upon me years ago by expressing your wish to have this subject painted, and I have never lost sight of the hope of obeying you. Ill done or well done, God

knows it is my best. The picture is
here."

He drew the easel round so that she
could see it without leaving her seat, and
while she looked upon it he turned away.
Strong emotion was making Montgomerie's pulses throb. Ingha's beauty, fragile, eloquently and exquisitely radiant,
though changed, was thrilling his soul
with unwonted and long-desired delight.

Ingha gazed on in silence; she at once
apprehended the likeness, but, as the spirit
of the work was gradually revealed, she
more and more disassociated it with herself, till at length only Saint Cecilia's
rapture and sorrow pervaded her thoughts.

Tears seemed ready to fall, for, weak and impressionable as she was, she could not altogether suppress them, and a sigh that was more like a stifled sob escaped her. Ruy, alert and strangely expectant, heard the sigh, and, turning to her, came to her side and said :

"Ingha, why do you weep ?"

"I do not know. Forgive me," she answered. "It is worth all the years of waiting to see this work of yours, but your poetic imaginings have transfigured my face into that which it could never become. I am changed indeed, for my art has gone from me. I shall never sing again, but "—she smiled through her tears—" I will try to grow glad through sorrowing, like sainted Cecilia."

"Oh, my Star, my Star," said Ruy, in a low tone, coming closer to her side, "do not so coldly gleam upon me. Ingha, you know, you must know that all my heart, my life, my work are yours; that all the labour of the years of the past, of the years to come, I count smallest service, if but one word of approval from you be won. I have no other desire, no lesser hope. Do not condemn what I have already done, lest my hand trembles as I essay that which may prove more worthy of your praise."

Ingha's face had become very pale while Montgomerie was speaking, the fervent feeling in his tones, and the intense earn-

estness of his words impressed her with
a vague knowledge that this was a great
crisis in both their lives, and she could
with difficulty repress the eager impulses
that made her heart throb and her brain
heavy with emotion. The white rose she
had brought, intending to leave as a token
of her visit, was crushed, and its leaves
had fallen. Ah! she thought, if he only
knew all the sorrow and trouble she had
borne for his sake; but, though she had
her story to relate, she was still resolute
in endeavouring, however feebly, to be a
Spartan.

"I must tell you some of my own experiences," she said, with a winning soft-
ness. "Yesterday I found I was as likely

to die as to live. A short time ago
I was very ill, and I think my late despondency has aggravated the weakness.
I determined to arrange my affairs before I told anyone how frail I felt, lest
some hard instructions should be enjoined
by the doctors. Then I was perplexed
to find an excuse for seeing you, till Lady
Kinaire came and described your picture
just at the moment I was longing for some
pretext, and, after all, the picture was a
true reason for coming, though, much as
I wanted to see it, I wanted more to come
and say good-bye to you."

Ruy was standing quite close to her
now, leaning against the wall, his arms
folded across his breast, the Montgomerie

courage fighting as best it could with a sudden dread, but Ingha's sweet face, tenderly appealing, with an unspeakable yearning for a look or a word to help her, overcame Ruy, and he put his hand to his brow, as if to consider his answer, but in reality to hide his emotion.

Standing beside her there was such a visible contrast between them, he so stalwart and strong, she so fair and delicate, but Ruy felt conscious of a love that was mighty enough to engender strength, and he thought the power of such love could overcome every hindrance to the joy for which they had both so patiently endured.

He was kneeling beside her now, and

looking into her face with eyes that told of undying love and longing.

"My Love! my Love! you shall not bid me farewell if I can win you. Oh, Ingha, think how I have waited all silently, with a devotion that for years has asked nothing till to-day. You could not leave me now you know that without you I should be powerless for evermore. Do you not remember it was the ' *visible* protection of my Saint Cecilia' that I once told you alone would satisfy me?" and Ruy tried to smile, though imploring so earnestly.

"Roderigue," Ingha said, softly, "how little you know of the times I have wondered if all your love were given to your art while I was faithful alone to you.

Have you not felt that I have ever loved you ?"

More than one dream of Ruy's life was finding fulfilment to-day, for his memory had long been haunted by the questions Ingha had just asked.

"Ah, my sweet Saint, I realise the truth at last, but you must prove now that you love me more than you love Death."

"Mio Caro, perhaps Death may love me more than Love."

"Ingha ! Ingha ! my own, my own, say again that you love me, that Death may be scared by the sacred might of your vow."

"I do love you, Roderigue," answered Ingha, slowly.

" Wad she tak her fond vow back ?

I trow, no, no !"

She smiled as she rose, and he lifted her hand and pressed it to his lips. Her face flushed as she looked down on her little gloved hands.

" They have both been kissed now," she said, and, holding up her right hand, added, " it is this one that has ever been triumphant since the night in the gallery at Kerinvean."

A wild and anxious yearning possessed Ruy to enfold her, to bear her away where the tenderness of his devotion alone should lure her back to health and rapture, but ever gentle, ever heedful of her pure feelings, he repressed the passionate words that were in his thoughts, for he perceived that the excitement of the interview was telling upon her strength.

"Ingha, my Star, you will let me come to you soon, and meanwhile we will dream of our love and of the life we shall live ere long?"

"Yes," she answered, with downcast eyelids, "but, Roderigue," and here she hesitated a moment, and then laid her hand gently on his arm, and looked wistfully into his face, "perhaps I shall only bring you Valerian's fate; he would never have known martyrdom save for Cecilia, and it would be martyrdom for us to be parted again."

"And but for her," Ruy answered,

gravely, " he would never have known any higher possibility of life than that which Pagan worship inspired, nor any victorious death save for Cecilia, nor would he have foreseen a divine immortality but through his martyrdom. He rejoiced in his fate as I rejoice in mine; since all of God Valerian knew was revealed to him by his love, so I willingly abide by all that your love may bring to my lot, whether life or death, loss or gain. I cherish the same hopes that were Valerian's, and, as Cecilia's love was his earthly crown, so your love has crowned me to-day."

He stooped and kissed her brow, and an awe, as if an unseen presence were between them, made them for some moments silent.

Then Ingha took Ruy's hand and raised it to her lips, and with a gleam of memory lighting up her features, that had become unspeakably mournful, she said :

"I do not think I should have come had it not been '*Morituri te Salutant!*' I was not prepared to have my life transfigured, and my heart filled with hope ; but will you send me away now, for I am very tired ?"

"You may go, my Love, but I cannot send you," Ruy answered, smiling still sadly.

"And have you been a Spartan, dear ?" asked Marie, as she drove the ponies home.

"No, darling, I failed in that, because my Roman offered to accept even martyrdom for my sake, and I found I did not need to be other than myself." And Ingha's hand sought Marie's, and Ruy's sister said, in a voice full of loving emotion:

"May God bless you both, and bring your desires to pass!"

CHAPTER XVI.

WINGS AND WAVES.

" A winged sound of joy, and love, and wonder,
  Which soars where Expectation never flew,
  Rending the veil of space and time asunder !
  One ocean feeds the clouds, and streams, and dew;
  One sun illumines heaven ; one spirit vast
  With life and love makes chaos ever new."

SHELLEY.

" Wings to find an immortality."

KEATS.

IS it from childhood those memories come,
or from the histories we have tried to

recall; the memories, borne on a gentle tide, of endless songs in which mingled the whisperings of joyous nereids who sported in buoyant glee on its far-off waves? And the halcyon birds brooded on the waters, and yearning eyes sought not in vain for visions of promise, even for " the wings of a dove covered with silver, and her feathers with yellow gold."

The remorseless billows of human impotence dash in anger against the impregnable shores of doom, and neither victory nor triumph is heard in their passionate fury. Memory ever wanders gladly back to a lonely sea where the last conscious kiss of the dying God of day crimsoned the wave, or the moaning surge waited in sullen gloom for the first streak of dawn.

Ah me ! that he who rehearses the lives and loves of his fellows should ever have grief for the unfailing burden of his romance and song.

The Zulu war wages fiercely, heroes on both sides fall thick and fast like leaves in an autumn wind, and many of their bravest deeds will never be chronicled save by the recording angels.

Daring, courageous, and reckless, Sir Dallas Gore fights and endures, the most hopeless defence only exhilarating his spirit, the longest marches never causing him to utter a complaint.

Notwithstanding that assegais are flung

all round him, and men whose wives and children at home are praying for their safety are killed in sickening numbers by aim that is unerring, he bears a charmed life, and ever leads where danger threatens thickest and death is likeliest to follow.

And Marie at Invean hears of his valour with glowing pride in her dead lover's friend. And she wonders sadly if he too shall find a grave on those fateful fields of Africa.

But soon he will return, and honours he has never desired, though he has earned them well, will then be showered upon him. Will he win the guerdon lacking which to him all other meed will prove paltry and vain?

The waves of Destiny roll on, and the wings of Fate are still fluttering. It rests alone with her whose fair blossoms of hope were early chilled by the withering winds of fickle Time, and the hopeless blight of a graceless Chance.

Methinks I hear still the echoes of nereids singing in a halcyon hour on a sunny sea.

Roderigue Montgomerie well knew that his inspiration would now never fail, nor his power grow less, and, when the art-patron who had begged him to forego the subject of saintship in his great picture offered him an unwonted price for the work, he sold it. Already he felt impelled to nobler design and to more immortal purpose. The tide of time had raised its angry surf, but the pitiless foam of the billows of doubt and self-mistrust had never hidden nor dimmed the pure shining of his star, and he knew that his beacon had at last halted over the "glorious port," the haven of his dreams, where even now he could descry the temple where they two should serve, the sanctuary of love and art whose windows all fronted the rising sun.

Fitfully the wings of Chance have flitted across the horizon of our story; ofttimes ominous and dark have been their passage, and the shrieks that the watchers heard were dull and dismal prophecies of woe;

but anon the same weary sentinels have seen the white, majestic pinions of

"Angels in strong level flight"

winging their homeward way over the mountains of despondency and the far-reaching valleys of toil, leaving a shining track in their wake that led to a sea of infinite rest.

Fleet were the steps of the lover as he hurried to the home of Ingha. Did he fear that the star his eyes now beheld would elude his vision after all? Did he dread that the dark waves of Destiny might even yet rise up between them?

"Roderigue," she said, "the longest

life for which we dare pray will be all too brief for our love and work."

"Ingha, why should your thoughts dwell on the shortness of time? The eternity of love knows no end. Life or death for either can be only a condition where our love shall increase."

"Ah, Roderigue," she answered, "when the golden thread that bound us together was broken, when my art seemed no longer a possible link to your life, I did not care how soon death came, but at length the old longing for love revived, and when I thought I should die I hastened to put my house in order. I had ever been bent on my fortune repairing your wrong, and so I arranged that my death should put you in possession of that which would aid you to fulfil wherein I had failed, for I knew you would devote everything to the service that we both loved. But since you have turned again to that sweet page of our lives that has been closed so long, I dread to leave you. You will not let me die now, Roderigue?"

For a few moments Montgomerie did not speak, he was trying to think of all the possibilities of the future, but the bliss of Ingha's presence made riot of dread and despondency, and exorcised the phantoms that fear had invoked.

"My Love! my Love!" he said, with

passionate earnestness, looking down on her fair face, which was radiant with eager hope, "will you come to me now, come to me to inspire my work, and to bless my efforts with your beauty and love? Will you consent to this brief wooing, knowing that all my life will be one glorious dream of devotion to you, my bride? Time *is* brief for art, Ingha, and they who elect to tread the aisles of its temple together must not loiter where the crowd waits, nor linger to ask its approval of their resolve."

The appeal was sudden and stern, but his soul was full of longing to possess her ere Death might forestall him; he felt so sure that love could vanquish Death, for scant is the remembrance of the shadow of the dark wings of the Invincible when eyes that have vainly gazed in vacant skies are at last dazzled by the glistening, snowy pinions of the dove of promise. Ruy eagerly watched Ingha as she, standing by his side, covered her face with her trembling hands.

The songs of the nereids come from a far distance still, the sky tells of a calm, the waves are all at rest, and the wings that have hovered and fluttered are folded in peace.

Anon the hands of Ingha fell by her side, and she looked upward with rapturous emotion and met Ruy's gaze as she murmured :

"I will go, my Love, wherever it seemeth best to you."

Time speeds on, and Chance is forgotten. No earthly influence will ever disturb the rare serenity which fills the lives of Ruy and Ingha, for their art is inspired by a love that is deathless, which now

> "Can no longer borrow
> Its hues from chance and change, dark children of
> to-morrow."

THE END.

LONDON : PRINTED BY DUNCAN MACDONALD, BLENHEIM HOUSE.

ERRATA.

BOOK I.

Page 7, line 14, *for* track *read* tract.

BOOK II.

Page 66, line 8, *for* forms always *read* forms being always.

,, 80, ,, 12, *for* its glorious port *read* his glorious port.

,, 85, ,, 5, *for* Fortune *read* Fortuna.

,, 153, ,, 1, *for* strange a story *read* a strange story.

,, 176, ,, 2, *for* silly *read* simple.

,, 180, ,, 5, *for* and he had *read* and that he had.

BOOK III.

Page 26, line 1, *for* merciful *read* Merciful.

MESSRS. HURST AND BLACKETT'S

LIST OF NEW WORKS.

MESSRS. HURST AND BLACKETT'S
LIST OF NEW WORKS.

A VISIT TO ABYSSINIA; an ACCOUNT OF TRAVEL
IN MODERN ETHIOPIA. By W. WINSTANLEY, late 4th (Queen's Own) Hussars. 2 vols. crown 8vo. 21s.

"Mr. Winstanley may be congratulated on having produced a capital record of travels, cast in a popular mould. The narrative is written in a lively and entertaining style, and abounds in capital character sketches of the men with whom the author was brought into contact."—*Athenæum.*

"Mr. Winstanley's volumes contain a very considerable quantity of fresh information."—*Academy.*

"These volumes are extremely readable, and supply a large amount of curious information about regions and people but little known."—*Literary World.*

"Mr. Winstanley's personal adventures are in themselves sufficiently amusing, and, did they stand alone, would be well worth reading; but he has much to say besides about the strange land he explored, and the inhabitants who live in it."—*Daily Telegraph.*

"We congratulate Mr Winstanley on having produced a very interesting narrative from his experiences during an adventure surrounded with perils."—*Globe.*

LIFE IN WESTERN INDIA. By Mrs. GUTHRIE,
Author of "Through Russia," "My Year in an Indian Fort," &c. 2 vols. crown 8vo, with Illustrations. 21s.

"This is a remarkable book, for the variety and brilliance of the pictures which it sets before us. Mrs. Guthrie is no ordinary observer. She has a keen eye for scenery, and can describe what she sees with much vividness. Then she is a botanist, at home in the vast variety of the Indian flora, something of an archæologist, and has more than an ordinary knowledge of Indian history; and she notes with a keen interest the life and character of the native population. Altogether this is a charming book, in which we can find no fault, except it be an embarrassing richness of matter which makes us feel that we have given no idea of it to our readers; we can only say. Let them judge for themselves."—*Pall Mall Gazette.*

"Mrs. Guthrie's 'Life in Western India' is worthy the graphic pen of this accomplished writer. Her familiarity with Indian life enables her to portray in faithful and vivid hues the character of Hindoo and Mohammedan tribes, noting the peculiarities of their social and religious traditions, and representing their personal habits and manners with picturesque fidelity."—*Daily Telegraph.*

"A most charming and delightful book."—*Home News for India.*

CATHARINE OF ARAGON, AND THE SOURCES
OF THE ENGLISH REFORMATION. Edited, from the French of ALBERT DU BOYS, with Notes by CHARLOTTE M. YONGE, Author of "The Heir of Redclyffe," &c. 2 vols. crown 8vo. 21s.

"This book is valuable as an able compendium of documents about Catharine, and also as a statement of the causes which led to the English Reformation. It should be read by all who want to take a comprehensive view of the period. Miss Yonge's work is thoroughly and conscientiously done."—*Graphic.*

"Even those who are well acquainted with Miss Strickland and Lingard may derive much additional information and renewed pleasure from M. Albert du Boys. We do not think that the labour of translation has been in vain in the case of the present work. Miss Yonge's well-deserved reputation would of itself be sufficient to give it currency."—*The Tablet.*

MY JOURNEY ROUND THE WORLD, via
CEYLON, NEW ZEALAND, AUSTRALIA, TORRES STRAITS, CHINA, JAPAN, AND THE UNITED STATES. By CAPTAIN S. H. JONES-PARRY, late 102nd Royal Madras Fusileers. 2 vols. crown 8vo. 21s.

"A very pleasant book of travel, well worth reading."—*Spectator.*

"A lively account of the author's experiences ashore and afloat, which is well worth reading."—*Daily News.*

"It is pleasant to follow Captain Jones-Parry on his journey round the world. He is full of life, sparkle, sunlight, and anecdote."—*Graphic.*

1

MESSRS. HURST AND BLACKETT'S
NEW WORKS—*Continued.*

ROYAL WINDSOR. By W. HEPWORTH DIXON.

Second Edition. Volumes I. and II. Demy 8vo. 30s.

CONTENTS OF VOLS. I. AND II.—Castle Hill, Norman Keep, First King's House, Lion Heart, Kingless Windsor, Windsor Won, Geoffrey Plantagenet, Windsor Lost, The Fallen Deputy, The Queen Mother, Maud de Braose, The Barons' War, Second King's House, Edward of Carnarvon, Perot de Gaveston, Isabel de France, Edward of Windsor, Crecy, Patron Saints. St. George, Society of St. George, Lady Salisbury, David King of Scots, Third King's House, Ballad Windsor, The Fair Countess, Richard of Bordeaux, Court Parties. Royal Favourites, Rehearsing for Windsor. In the Great Hall, Simon de Burley, Radcote Bridge, A Feast of Death, Geoffrey Chaucer, At Winchester Tower. St. George's Chapel, The Little Queen, At Windsor, Duchess Philippote, The Windsor Plot, Bolingbroke, Court of Chivalry, Wager of Battle, Captive Little Queen, A New Year's Plot, Night of the Kings, Dona Juana, Constance of York, The Norman Tower, The Legal Heir. Prince Hal, The Devil's Tower, In Captivity Captive. Attempt at Rescue, Agincourt, Kaiser Sigismund, The Witch Queen, Sweet Kate, The Maid of Honour, Lady Jane, Henry of Windsor, Richard of York, Two Duchesses, York and Lancaster, Union of the Roses.

"'Royal Windsor' follows in the same lines as 'Her Majesty's Tower,' and aims at weaving a series of popular sketches of striking events which centre round Windsor Castle. Mr. Dixon makes everything vivid and picturesque. Those who liked 'Her Majesty's Tower' will find these volumes equally pleasant."—*Athenæum.*

"A truly fine and interesting book. It is a valuable contribution to English history; worthy of Mr. Dixon's fame, worthy of its grand subject."—*Morning Post.*

"Mr. Dixon has supplied us with a highly entertaining book. 'Royal Windsor' is eminently a popular work, bristling with anecdotes and amusing sketches of historical characters. It is carefully written, and is exceedingly pleasant reading. The story is brightly told; not a dull page can be found."—*Examiner.*

"These volumes will find favour with the widest circle of readers. From the first days of Norman Windsor to the Plantagenet period Mr. Dixon tells the story of this famous castle in his own picturesque, bright, and vigorous way."—*Daily Telegraph.*

"Mr. Hepworth Dixon has found a congenial subject in 'Royal Windsor.' Under the sanction of the Queen, he has enjoyed exceptional opportunities of most searching and complete investigation of the Royal House and every other part of Windsor Castle, in and out, above ground and below ground."—*Daily News.*

VOLS. III. AND IV. OF ROYAL WINDSOR. By

W. HEPWORTH DIXON. *Second Edition.* Demy 8vo. 30s. Completing the Work.

CONTENTS OF VOLS. III. AND IV.—St. George's Hall, The Tudor Tower, A Windsor Comedy, The Secret Room, Treaties of Windsor, The Private Stair, Disgrading a Knight, In a King's House, The Maiden's Tower. Black Days. The Virgin Bride, Elegy on Windsor, Fair Geraldine, Course of Song. A Windsor Gospeller, Windsor Martyrs, A Royal Reference, Hatchment Down, The People's Friend, St. George's Enemy, Lady Elizabeth's Grace, Queen Mary, Grand Master of St. George, Deanery and Dean, Sister Temperance, Elizabeth's Lovers, Dudley Constable, The Schoolmaster, Peace, Proclaimed, Shakespere's Windsor, The Two Shakesperes, The Merry Wives, Good Queen Bess, House of Stuart, The Little Park, The Queen's Court, The King's Knights, Spurious Peace. King Christian, A Catholic Dean, Apostasy, Expulsion, Forest Rights, Book of Sports, Windsor Cross, In the Forest, Windsor Seized, Under the Keep, At Bay, Feudal Church. Roundheads. Cavalier Prisoners, The New Model, Last Days of Royalty, Saints in Council, Changing Sides, Bagshot Lodge. Cutting Down, Windsor Uncrowned, A "Merry" Cæsar, Windsor Catholic, The Catastrophe, Domestic Life, Home.

"Readers of all classes will feel a genuine regret to think that these volumes contain the last of Mr. Dixon's vivid and lively sketches of English history. His hand retained its cunning to the last, and these volumes show an increase in force and dignity."—*Athenæum.*

"Mr. Dixon's is the picturesque way of writing history. Scene after scene is brought before us in the most effective way. His book is not only pleasant reading, but full of information."—*Graphic.*

2

MESSRS. HURST AND BLACKETT'S
NEW WORKS—*Continued.*

CONVERSATIONS WITH DISTINGUISHED PERSONS

during the Second Empire, from 1860 to 1863. By the Late NASSAU W. SENIOR. Edited by his Daughter, M. C. M. SIMPSON. 2 vols. 8vo. 30s.

Among other persons whose conversations are given in these volumes are:—Prince Napoleon; the Duc de Broglie; the Marquises Chambrun, Lastcyrie, Palla-vicini, Vogué; Marshal Randon; Counts Arrivabene, Circourt, Corcelle, Ker-gorlay, Montalembert, Rémusat, Zamoyski; Generals Changarnier, Fénélon, Trochu; Lords Cowley and Clyde; Messieurs Ampère, Beaumont, Chambol, Chevalier, Cousin, Dayton, Drouyn de Lhuys, Duchâtel, Dufaure, Dumon, Duvergier de Hauranne, Guizot, Lamartine, Loménie, Lavergne, Lanjuinais, Maury, Marochetti, Masson, Mérimée, Odillon Barrot, Pelletan, Pietri, Rénan, St. Hilaire, Slidell, Thiers, De Witt; Mesdames Circourt, Cornu, Mohl, &c.

"Mr. Senior's 'Conversations with M. Thiers, M. Guizot,' &c., published about a year and a half ago, were the most interesting volumes of the series which had appeared up to that time, and these new 'Conversations' are hardly, if at all, less welcome and important. A large part of this delightful book is made up of studies by various critics, from divers points of view, of the character of Louis Napoleon, and of more or less vivid and accurate explanations of his tortuous policy. The work contains a few extremely interesting reports of conversations with M. Thiers. There are some valuable reminiscences of Lamartine, and among men of a some-what later day, of Prince Napoleon, Drouyn de Lhuys, Montalembert, Victor Cousin, Rénan, and the Chevaliers."—*Athenæum.*

"It is impossible to do justice to these 'Conversations' in a brief notice, so we must be content to refer our readers to volumes which, wherever they are opened, will be found pregnant with interest."—*The Times.*

"Many readers may prefer the dramatic or literary merit of Mr. Senior's 'Con-versations' to their historical interest, but it is impossible to insert extracts of such length as to represent the spirit, the finish, and the variety of a book which is throughout entertaining and instructive."—*Saturday Review.*

CONVERSATIONS WITH M. THIERS, M. GUIZOT,

and other Distinguished Persons, during the Second Empire. By the Late NASSAU W. SENIOR. Edited by his Daughter, M. C. M. SIMPSON. 2 vols. demy 8vo. 30s.

Among other persons whose conversations are recorded in these volumes are:— King Leopold; the Duc de Broglie; Lord Cowley; Counts Arrivabene, Cor-celle, Daru, Flahault, Kergolay, Montalembert; Generals Lamoricière and Chrzanowski; Sir Henry Ellis; Messieurs Ampère, Beaumont, Blanchard, Bouffet, Auguste Chevalier, Victor Cousin, De Witt, Duchâtel, Ducpetiaux, Dumon, Dussard, Duvergier de Hauranne, Léon Faucher, Frère-Orban, Grim-blot, Guizot, Lafitte, Labaume, Lamartine, Lanjuinais, Mallac, Mauin, Mérimée, Mignet, Jules Mohl, Montanelli, Odillon-Barrot, Quêtelet, Rémusat, Rogier, Rivet, Rossini, Horace Say, Thiers, Trouvé-Chauvel, Villemain, Wolowski; Mesdames Circourt, Cornu, Ristori, &c.

"This new series of Mr. Senior's 'Conversations' has been for some years past known in manuscript to his more intimate friends, and it has always been felt that no former series would prove more valuable or important. Mr. Senior had a social position which gave him admission into the best literary and political circles of Paris. He was a cultivated and sensible man, who knew how to take full advan-tage of such an opening. And above all, he had by long practice so trained his memory as to enable it to recall all the substance, and often the words, of the long conversations which he was always holding. These conversations he wrote down with a surprising accuracy, and then handed the manuscript to his friends, that they might correct or modify his report of what they had said. This book thus contains the opinions of eminent men given in the freedom of conversation, and afterwards carefully revised. Of their value there cannot be a question. The book is one of permanent historical interest. There is scarcely a page without some memorable statement by some memorable man. Politics and society and literature —the three great interests that make up life—are all discussed in turn, and there is no discussion which is unproductive of weighty thought or striking fact."—*Athenæum.*

3

MESSRS. HURST AND BLACKETT'S
NEW WORKS—*Continued.*

HISTORY OF TWO QUEENS: CATHARINE
OF ARAGON and ANNE BOLEYN. By W. HEPWORTH DIXON.
Second Edition. Vols. 1 & 2. Demy 8vo. 30s.

"In two handsome volumes Mr. Dixon here gives us the first instalment of a new historical work on a most attractive subject. The book is in many respects a favourable specimen of Mr. Dixon's powers. It is the most painstaking and elaborate that he has yet written. . . . . On the whole, we may say that the book is one which will sustain the reputation of its author as a writer of great power and versatility, that it gives a new aspect to many an old subject, and presents in a very striking light some of the most recent discoveries in English history."—*Athenæum.*

"In these volumes the author exhibits in a signal manner his special powers and finest endowments. It is obvious that the historian has been at especial pains to justify his reputation, to strengthen his hold upon the learned, and also to extend his sway over the many who prize an attractive style and interesting narrative more highly than laborious research and philosophic insight."—*Morning Post.*

"The thanks of all students of English history are due to Mr. Hepworth Dixon for his clever and original work, 'History of two Queens.' The book is a valuable contribution to English history."—*Daily News.*

VOLS. III. & IV. OF THE HISTORY OF TWO
QUEENS: CATHARINE OF ARAGON and ANNE BOLEYN.
By W. HEPWORTH DIXON. *Second Edition.* Demy 8vo. Price 30s.
Completing the Work.

"These concluding volumes of Mr. Dixon's 'History of two Queens' will be perused with keen interest by thousands of readers. Whilst no less valuable to the student, they will be far more enthralling to the general reader than the earlier half of the history. Every page of what may be termed Anne Boleyn's story affords a happy illustration of the author's vivid and picturesque style. The work should be found in every library."—*Post.*

HISTORY OF WILLIAM PENN, Founder of
Pennsylvania. By W. HEPWORTH DIXON. A NEW LIBRARY EDITION
1 vol. demy 8vo, with Portrait. 12s.

"Mr. Dixon's 'William Penn' is, perhaps, the best of his books. He has now revised and issued it with the addition of much fresh matter. It is now offered in a sumptuous volume, matching with Mr. Dixon's recent books, to a new generation of readers, who will thank Mr. Dixon for his interesting and instructive memoir of one of the worthies of England."—*Examiner.*

VOLS. III. & IV. OF HER MAJESTY'S TOWER.
By W. HEPWORTH DIXON. DEDICATED BY EXPRESS
PERMISSION TO THE QUEEN. Completing the Work. *Third
Edition.* Demy 8vo. 30s.

FREE RUSSIA. By W. HEPWORTH DIXON. *Third*
Edition. 2 vols. 8vo, with Coloured Illustrations. 30s.

"Mr. Dixon's book will be certain not only to interest but to please its readers and it deserves to do so. It contains a great deal that is worthy of attention, and is likely to produce a very useful effect."—*Saturday Review.*

THE SWITZERS. By W. HEPWORTH DIXON.
Third Edition. 1 vol. demy 8vo. 15s.

"A lively, interesting, and altogether novel book on Switzerland. It is full of valuable information on social, political, and ecclesiastical questions, and, like all Mr. Dixon's books, is eminently readable."—*Daily News.*

MESSRS. HURST AND BLACKETT'S
NEW WORKS—Continued.

OUR HOLIDAY IN THE EAST. By Mrs. GEORGE
SUMNER. Edited by the Rev. G. H. SUMNER, Hon. Canon of Winchester, Rector of Old Alresford, Hants. SECOND AND CHEAPER EDITION. One vol. crown 8vo, with Illustrations. 6s. bound.

"'Our Holiday in the East' may take its place among the earnest and able books recording personal travel and impressions in those lands which are consecrated to us by their identification with Bible history."—*Daily Telegraph.*

"A most charming narrative of a tour in the East amongst scenes of the deepest interest to the Christian. No one can rise from the perusal of this fascinating volume without the pleasant conviction of having obtained much valuable aid for the study of the inspired narrative of Our Blessed Lord's life."—*Record.*

"An attractive volume, which is very agreeable reading."—*John Bull.*

DIARY OF A TOUR IN SWEDEN, NORWAY,
AND RUSSIA, IN 1827. By THE MARCHIONESS OF WESTMINSTER. 1 vol. demy 8vo. 15s.

"A bright and lively record. So pleasantly are the letters written which Lady Westminster sent home, that her book is most agreeable; and it has this special merit, that it brings clearly before us a number of the great people of former days, royal and imperial personages, whose intimate acquaintance the traveller's rank enabled her to make."—*Athenæum.*

"A very agreeable and instructive volume."—*Saturday Review.*

TALES OF OUR GREAT FAMILIES. Second
Series. By EDWARD WALFORD, M.A. 2 vols. crown 8vo. 21s.

CONTENTS:—The Old Countess of Desmond, The Edgcumbes of Edgcumbe and Cothole, The Lynches of Galway, A Cadet of the Plantagenets, The Proud Duke of Somerset, Lady Kilsyth, The Dalzells of Carnwath, The Ladies of Llangollen, The Foxes, The Stuarts of Traquair, Belted Will Howard, An Episode in the House of Dundonald, The Ducal House of Hamilton, The Chief of Dundas, The Duke of Chandos and Princely Canons, The Spencers and Comptons, All the Howards, The Lockharts of Lee, A Ghost Story in the Noble House of Beresford, A Tragedy in Pull Mall, An Eccentric Russell, The Lady of Lathom House, Two Royal Marriages in the Last Century, The Boyles, The Merry Duke of Montagu, The Romance of the Earldom of Huntingdon, Lady Hester Stanhope, The Countess of Nithsdale, The Romance of the Earldom of Mar, Margaret Duchess of Newcastle, Lord Northington, The Cutlers of Wentworth, The Earldom of Bridgewater, The Carews of Beddington, A Chapter on the Peerage, The Kirkpatricks of Closeburn, The Cliffords Earls of Cumberland, The Homes of Polwarth. The Ducal House of Bedford, Tragedies of the House of Innes, The Ducal House of Leinster, The Royal House of Stuart, The Great Douglas Case, The Radcliffes of Derwentwater, The Rise of the House of Hardwicke, Field-Marshal Keith.

"The social rank of the persons whose lives and characters are delineated in this work and the inherent romance of the stories it embodies will ensure it a widespread popularity. Many of the papers possess an engrossing and popular interest, while all of them may be read with pleasure and profit."—*Examiner.*

PLAYS, PLAYERS, AND PLAYHOUSES, AT
HOME AND ABROAD; WITH ANECDOTES OF THE DRAMA AND THE STAGE. By LORD WILLIAM PITT LENNOX. 2 vols. crown 8vo. 21s.

"Lord William Lennox's gossiping volumes will be read with great interest. They embrace notes concerning Peg Woffington, Mrs. Jordan, G. F. Cooke, the Infant Roscius, T. P. Cooke, Mrs. Honey, Romeo Coates, Alfred Bunn, the Kembles, Edmund Kean, Liston, Braham, Young, Grimaldi, Mrs. Billington, Morton, Colman, Planché, Sheridan Knowles, Theodore Hook, Mark Lemon, Palgrave Simpson, Byron, Burnand, Arthur Cecil Toole, Corney Grain, Irving, and many others. A vast amount of curious information and anecdote has been gathered together in these pleasant, readable volumes."—*Sunday Times.*

"These volumes are full of good stories and anecdotes, told with remarkable spirit, and will be a treasure to playgoers."—*Graphic.*

"The lover of the stage will find a host of interesting and amusing passages, let him dip into these volumes wherever he will."—*Era.*

MESSRS. HURST AND BLACKETT'S
NEW WORKS—*Continued.*

MONSIEUR GUIZOT IN PRIVATE LIFE (1787-
1874). By His Daughter, Madame DE WITT. Translated by Mrs.
SIMPSON. 1 vol. demy 8vo. 15s.

"Madame de Witt has done justice to her father's memory in an admirable record of his life. Mrs. Simpson's translation of this singularly interesting book is in accuracy and grace worthy of the original and of the subject."—*Saturday Review.*

"This book was well worth translating. Mrs. Simpson has written excellent English, while preserving the spirit of the French."—*The Times.*

"M. Guizot stands out in the pages of his daughter's excellent biography a distinct and life-like figure. He is made to speak to us in his own person. The best part of the book consists of a number of his letters, in which he freely unfolds his feelings and opinions, and draws with unconscious boldness the outlines of his forcible and striking character."—*Pall Mall Gazette.*

THE VILLAGE OF PALACES; or, Chronicles of
Chelsea. By the Rev. A. G. L'ESTRANGE. 2 vols. crown 8vo. 21s.

"Mr. L'Estrange has much to tell of the various public institutions associated with Chelsea. Altogether his volumes show some out-of-the-way research, and are written in a lively and gossipping style."—*The Times.*

"These volumes are pleasantly written and fairly interesting."—*Athenæum.*

"Mr. L'Estrange tells us much that is interesting about Chelsea. We take leave of this most charming book with a hearty recommendation of it to our readers."—*Spectator.*

"One of the best gossiping topographies since Leigh Hunt's 'Old Court Suburb.' So many persons of note have lived in Chelsea that a book far less carefully compiled than this has been could not fail to be amusing."—*Daily Telegraph.*

"Every inhabitant of Chelsea will welcome this remarkably interesting work. It sheds a flood of light upon the past; and, while avoiding the heaviness of most antiquarian works, gives, in the form of a popular and amusing sketch, a complete history of this 'Village of Palaces.'"—*Chelsea News*

AN ACTOR ABROAD; or, GOSSIP, DRAMATIC,
NARRATIVE, AND DESCRIPTIVE: From the Recollections of an Actor in Australia, New Zealand, the Sandwich Islands, California, Nevada, Central America, and New York. By EDMUND LEATHES. Demy 8vo. 15s.

"'An Actor Abroad' is a bright and pleasant volume—an eminently readable book. Mr. Leathes has the great merit of being never dull. He has the power of telling a story clearly and pointedly."—*Saturday Review.*

"A readable, gossipping, agreeable record."—*Era.*

RORAIMA AND BRITISH GUIANA, with a
Glance at Bermuda, the West Indies, and the Spanish Main. By J. W. BODDAM-WHETHAM. 8vo. With Map and Illustrations. 15s.

"The author has succeeded in producing an interesting and readable book of travels. His remarks on every-day life in the tropics, his notes on the geography and natural history of the countries he visited, and, above all, his vivid descriptions of scenery, combine to form a record of adventure which in attractiveness it will not be easy to surpass."—*Athenæum.*

"Mr. Whetham travelled in portions of Guiana little known, meeting with many adventures, seeing many strange sights, and taking notes which have furnished matter for a book of fascinating interest."—*Daily News.*

CELEBRITIES I HAVE KNOWN. By LORD
WILLIAM PITT LENNOX. *Second Series.* 2 volumes demy 8vo. 30s.

"This new series of Lord William Lennox's reminiscences is fully as entertaining as the preceding one. Lord William makes good use of an excellent memory, and he writes easily and pleasantly."—*Pall Mall Gazette.*

MESSRS. HURST AND BLACKETT'S
NEW WORKS—*Continued.*

HOLIDAYS IN EASTERN FRANCE; Sketches
of Travel in CHAMPAGNE, FRANCHE-COMTE, the JURA, the VALLEY of the DOUBS, &c. By M. BETHAM-EDWARDS. 8vo. Illustrations. 15s.

"Miss Edwards' present volume, written in the same pleasant style as that which described her wanderings in Western France, is so much the more to be recommended that its contents are fresher and more novel."—*Saturday Review.*

"Readers of this work will find plenty of fresh information about some of the most delightful parts of France. The descriptions of scenery are as graphic as the sketches of character are lifelike."—*Globe.*

ROUND THE WORLD IN SIX MONTHS. By
LIEUT.-COLONEL E. S. BRIDGES, Grenadier Guards. 1 vol. 8vo. 15s.

"The author may be congratulated on his success, for his pages are light and pleasant. The volume will be found both amusing and useful."—*Athenæum.*

"Colonel Bridges' book has the merit of being lively and readable. His advice to future travellers may be found serviceable."—*Pall Mall Gazette.*

A LEGACY: Being the Life and Remains of JOHN
MARTIN, Schoolmaster and Poet. Written and Edited by the Author of "JOHN HALIFAX." 2 vols. crown 8vo. With Portrait. 21s.

"A remarkable book. It records the life, work, aspirations, and death of a schoolmaster and poet, of lowly birth but ambitious soul. His writings brim with vivid thought, touches of poetic sentiment, and trenchant criticism of men and books, expressed in scholarly language."—*Guardian.*

"Mrs. Craik has related a beautiful and pathetic story—a story of faith and courage on the part of a young and gifted man, who might under other circumstances have won a place in literature. The story is one worth reading."—*Pall Mall Gazette.*

LIFE OF MOSCHELES; WITH SELECTIONS FROM
HIS DIARIES AND CORRESPONDENCE. By HIS WIFE.
2 vols. large post 8vo, with Portrait. 24s.

"This life of Moscheles will be a valuable book of reference for the musical historian, for the contents extend over a period of threescore years, commencing with 1794, and ending at 1870. We need scarcely state that all the portions of Moscheles' diary which refer to his intercourse with Beethoven, Hummel, Weber, Czerny, Spontini, Rossini, Auber, Halévy, Schumann, Cherubini, Spohr, Mendelssohn, F. David, Chopin, J B. Cramer, Clementi, John Field, Habeneck, Hauptmann, Kalkbrenner, Kiesewetter, O. Klingemann, Lablache, Dragonetti, Sontag, Persiani, Malibran, Paganini, Rachel, Ronzi de Begnis, De Beriot, Ernst, Donzelli, Cinti-Damoreau, Chelard, Bochsa, Laporte, Charles Kemble, Paton (Mrs. Wood), Schröder-Devrient, Mrs. Siddons, Sir H. Bishop, Sir G. Smart, Staudigl, Thalberg, Berlioz, Velluti, C. Young, Balfe, Braham, and many other artists of note in their time, will recall a flood of recollections. It was a delicate task for Madame Moscheles to select from the diaries in reference to living persons, but her extracts have been judiciously made. Moscheles writes fairly of what is called the ' Music of the Future ' and its disciples, and his judgments on Herr Wagner, Dr. Liszt, Rubenstein, Dr. von Bülow, Litolff, &c., whether as composers or executants, are in a liberal spirit. He recognizes cheerfully the talents of our native artists; Sir S. Bennett, Mr. Macfarren, Madame Goddard, Mr. J. Barnett, Mr. Hullah, Mr. A. Sullivan, &c. The volumes are full of amusing anecdotes."—*Athenæum.*

COACHING ; With ANECDOTES OF THE ROAD. By
LORD WILLIAM PITT LENNOX. Dedicated to His Grace the DUKE OF BEAUFORT, K.G., President, and the Members of the Coaching Club. 1 vol. demy 8vo. 15s.

"Lord William's book is genial, discursive, and gossipy. We are indebted to the author's personal recollections for some lively stories, and pleasant sketches of some of the more famous dragsmen. Altogether his volume, with the variety of its contents, will be found pleasant reading."—*Pall Mall Gazette.*

MESSRS. HURST AND BLACKETT'S
NEW WORKS—*Continued.*

WORDS OF HOPE AND COMFORT TO
THOSE IN SORROW. Dedicated by Permission to THE QUEEN.
Fourth Edition. 1 vol. small 4to, 5s. bound.

"These letters, the work of a pure and devout spirit, deserve to find many readers. They are greatly superior to the average of what is called religious literature."—*Athenæum.*

"The writer of the tenderly-conceived letters in this volume was Mrs. Julius Hare, a sister of Mr. Maurice. They are instinct with the devout submissiveness and fine sympathy which we associate with the name of Maurice; but in her there is added a winningness of tact, and sometimes, too, a directness of language, which we hardly find even in the brother. The letters were privately printed and circulated, and were found to be the source of much comfort, which they cannot fail to afford now to a wide circle. A sweetly-conceived memorial poem, bearing the well-known initials, 'E. H. P.', gives a very faithful outline of the life."—*British Quarterly Review.*

"This touching and most comforting work is dedicated to THE QUEEN, who took a gracious interest in its first appearance, when printed for private circulation, and found comfort in its pages, and has now commanded its publication, that the world in general may profit by it. A more practical and heart-stirring appeal to the afflicted we have never examined."—*Standard.*

THE YOUTH OF QUEEN ELIZABETH. Edited,
from the French of L. WIESENER, by CHARLOTTE M. YONGE, Author
of "The Heir of Redclyffe," &c. 2 vols. crown 8vo. 21s.

"M. Wiesener is to be complimented on the completeness, accuracy, and research shown in this work. He has drawn largely on the French Archives, the Public Record Office, and British Museum, for information contained in original documents, to some of which notice is directed for the first time. M. Wiesener's work is well worth translating. Miss Yonge appears to have successfully accomplished the task which she has undertaken."—*Athenæum.*

THE SEA OF MOUNTAINS: AN ACCOUNT OF
LORD DUFFERIN'S TOUR THROUGH BRITISH COLUMBIA IN 1876. By
MOLYNEUX ST. JOHN. 2 vols. With Portrait of Lord Dufferin. 21s.

A YOUNG SQUIRE OF THE SEVENTEENTH
CENTURY, from the Papers of CHRISTOPHER JEAFFRESON, of Dullingham House, Cambridgeshire. Edited by JOHN CORDY JEAFFRESON, Author of "A Book about Doctors," &c. 2 vols. crown 8vo. 21s.

OUR BISHOPS AND DEANS. By the Rev. F.
ARNOLD, B.A., late of Christ Church, Oxford. 2 vols. 8vo. 30s.

LIFE OF THE RT. HON. SPENCER PERCEVAL;
Including His Correspondence. By His Grandson, SPENCER WALPOLE. 2 vols. 8vo. With Portrait. 30s.

HISTORIC CHATEAUX: BLOIS, FONTAINEBLEAU,
VINCENNES. By LORD LAMINGTON. 1 vol. 8vo. 15s.

"A very interesting volume."—*Times.*

THE THEATRE FRANCAIS IN THE REIGN
OF LOUIS XV. By LORD LAMINGTON. 1 vol. demy 8vo. 15s.

RECOLLECTIONS OF COLONEL DE GONNE-
VILLE. Edited from the French by CHARLOTTE M. YONGE,
Author of the "Heir of Redclyffe," &c. 2 vols. crown 8vo. 21s.

MESSRS, HURST AND BLACKETT'S
NEW WORKS—*Continued.*

A CHRISTIAN WOMAN. Being the Life of MA-
DAME JULES MALLET, *née* OBERKAMPF. By MADAME DE WITT, *née*
GUIZOT. Translated by Mrs. H. N. GOODHART. With a Preface
by the Author of "John Halifax, Gentleman." One vol. Foolscap
8vo. 5s.

MEMOIRS OF GEORGIANA, LADY CHATTER-
TON; With some Passages from her Diary. By E. HENEAGE
DERING. 1 vol. demy 8vo. 15s.

HISTORY OF ENGLISH HUMOUR. By the
Rev. A. G. L'ESTRANGE. 2 vols. crown 8vo. 21s.

A MAN OF OTHER DAYS: Recollections of the
MARQUIS DE BEAUREGARD. Edited, from the French, by CHARLOTTE
M. YONGE, Author of "The Heir of Redclyffe," &c. 2 vols. 21s.

MY YEAR IN AN INDIAN FORT. By Mrs.
GUTHRIE. 2 vols. crown 8vo. With Illustrations. 21s.

THROUGH FRANCE AND BELGIUM, BY
RIVER AND CANAL, IN THE STEAM YACHT "YTENE."
By W. J. C. MOENS, R.V.Y.C. 1 vol. 8vo. With Illustrations. 15s.

MY YOUTH, BY SEA AND LAND, FROM 1809 TO
1816. By CHARLES LOFTUS, formerly of the Royal Navy,
late of the Coldstream Guards. 2 vols. crown 8vo. 21s.

MY LIFE, FROM 1815 TO 1849. By CHARLES LOFTUS,
formerly of the Royal Navy, late of the Coldstream Guards.
Author of "My Youth by Sea and Land." 2 vols. crown 8vo. 21s.

A BOOK ABOUT THE TABLE. By J. C.
JEAFFRESON. 2 vols. 8vo. 30s.

COSITAS ESPANOLAS; OR, EVERY-DAY LIFE IN
SPAIN. By Mrs. HARVEY, of Ickwell-Bury. 2nd Edition. 8vo. 15s.

PEARLS OF THE PACIFIC. By J. W. BODDAM-
WHETHAM. 1 vol. demy 8vo, with 8 Illustrations. 15s.

TURKISH HAREMS & CIRCASSIAN HOMES.
By MRS. HARVEY, of Ickwell-Bury. 8vo. *Second Edition.* 15s.

MEMOIRS OF QUEEN HORTENSE, MOTHER
OF NAPOLEON III. Cheaper Edition, in 1 vol. 6s.

RECOLLECTIONS OF SOCIETY IN FRANCE
AND ENGLAND. By LADY CLEMENTINA DAVIES. 2nd Edition. 2 v.

THE EXILES AT ST. GERMAINS. By the
Author of "The Ladye Shakerley." 1 vol. 7s. 6d. bound.

9

THE NEW AND POPULAR NOVELS.
PUBLISHED BY HURST & BLACKETT.

SOPHY : OR, THE ADVENTURES OF A SAVAGE. By VIOLET FANE, Author of "The Edwin and Angelina Papers," "Denzil Place," &c. SECOND EDITION. 3 vols.

LITTLE FIFINE. By Mrs. MACQUOID, Author of "Patty," "Beside the River," &c. 3 vols.

TILL DEATH US DO PART. By Mrs. J. K. SPENDER, Author of "Godwyn's Ordeal," &c. 3 vols.

MISS DAISY DIMITY. By the Author of "Queenie," "A Jewel of a Girl," &c. 3 vols.

TOO FAST TO LAST. By JOHN MILLS, Author of "The Old English Gentleman," &c. 3 vols.
"The author of 'The Old English Gentleman' has produced another novel which will bear favourable comparison with its predecessor. It is an interesting story, full of life and incident."—*Sunday Times.*

IVY : COUSIN AND BRIDE. By PERCY GREG, Author of "Errant," &c. 3 vols.
"'Ivy' can be recommended pretty strongly to persons who are able to recognise accurate drawing of character, and still more strongly to those who appreciate pathos."—*Saturday Review.*
"'Ivy' is based upon a really original situation, which is not only made interesting, but receives the stamp of apparent reality."—*Globe.*
"A very cleverly-imagined story, cleverly told. A more charming heroine than Ivy has rarely been introduced to the world of readers."—*Morning Advertiser.*
"There are some clever sketches of journalistic life and character in 'Ivy.'"—*Academy.*

WANTED, AN HEIR. By C. L. PIRKIS, Author of "A Very Opal," &c. 3 vols.
"A pleasant and interesting novel."—*St. James's Gazette.*
"Mrs. Pirkis has given us a story with a fresh and unconventional heroine. The novel is exceedingly interesting."—*Academy.*
"A thoroughly interesting, original, and well-written story."—*John Bull.*

SYDNEY. By GEORGIANA M. CRAIK, Author of "Dorcas," "Anne Warwick," &c. 3 vols.
"There is much to commend in this novel. It is a very pretty story, cleverly devised, and wholesomely carried out."—*Saturday Review.*
"'Sydney' is one of the best of Miss Craik's novels. It is a well-written, pleasant story, and a highly interesting study of character."—*St. James's Gazette.*

RESEDA. By Mrs. RANDOLPH, Author of "Gentianella," &c. 3 vols.
"There is much that is clever in this story, both in the way of character-painting and incident."—*John Bull.*
"'Reseda' is pleasant to read, and will sustain its author's reputation. It is calculated to give a good deal of pleasure to lovers of modern fiction."—*Post.*

LOVE, HONOUR, AND OBEY. By IZA DUFFUS HARDY, Author of "Glencairn," &c. 3 vols.
"A very clever story. It is likely to attract many readers."—*John Bull.*
"A story of strong interest and power."—*Post.*
"The best novel Miss Hardy has written. The interest is steadily maintained to the end."—*Sunday Times.*

THE NEW AND POPULAR NOVELS.

PUBLISHED BY HURST & BLACKETT.

A MAN'S MISTAKE. By the Author of "St.
Olave's," "Janita's Cross," &c. 3 vols.
"'A Man's Mistake,' like the other novels by the same author, is written in a
pleasant style."—*Athenæum.*
"A carefully-executed study of provincial life in the well-known style of the
author of 'St. Olave's.' The character-painting is admirably done."—*Academy.*
"This novel is well-written and pleasant to read."—*Graphic.*

HARRY JOSCELYN. By Mrs. OLIPHANT, Author
of "Chronicles of Carlingford," &c. 3 vols.
"In 'Harry Joscelyn' Mrs. Oliphant makes judicious use of sharp and telling
contrasts. Nothing can be better than her pictures of the bleak Cumberland fells
and their rough inhabitants, except her clever sketches of Anglo-Italian life in
Leghorn. Harry himself is a clever and interesting study."—*The Times.*
"This book is very clever and entertaining. The characters are good, and every
page abounds in those little touches of true and subtle observation in which Mrs.
Oliphant excels."—*Pall Mall Gazette.*
"Mrs. Oliphant presents in these volumes a succession of studies, worked out
with great care, and evidencing her own peculiar skill."—*Saturday Review.*

AMONG THE HILLS. By E. FRANCES POYNTER,
Author of "My Little Lady," &c. 2 vols.
"Miss Poynter has undoubted power. She showed this in her first novel, 'My
Little Lady'; she has proved it yet again in her new venture, which is, moreover,
a distinct advance upon its predecessor. For depth and sincerity of feeling, quiet
pathos, and good taste, 'Among the Hills' may take rank among the better-class
fictions of the day."—*St. James's Gazette.*
"A touching and powerful story."—*Spectator.*

HIS LITTLE MOTHER, and Other Tales and
Sketches. By the Author of "JOHN HALIFAX." 1 vol. 10s. 6d.
"This is an interesting book, written in a pleasant manner, and full of shrewd
observation and kindly feeling. It is a book that will be read with interest, and
that cannot be lightly forgotten."—*St. James's Gazette.*
"'His Little Mother' is one of those pathetic stories which the author tells
better than anybody else."—*John Bull.*

STRICTLY TIED UP. By the RIGHT HON. A. J. B.
BERESFORD HOPE, M.P. *Third and Cheaper Edition.* 1 vol. 6s.
"A clever story. In 'Strictly Tied Up' we have vigorous sketches of life in
very different circumstances and conditions. We have the incisive portraiture of
character that shows varied knowledge of mankind. We have a novel, besides,
which may be read with profit as well as pleasure, for the author deals occasion-
ally with burning topics of the day."—*The Times.*

THE FUTURE MARQUIS. By CATHARINE
CHILDAR. 3 vols.
"An interesting story, written in an agreeable manner. It ought to attain con-
siderable popularity."—*John Bull.*

LOVE-KNOTS. By the Author of "Ursula's Love
Story," "Under Temptation," &c. 3 vols.
"There is a good deal of interest in these cleverly-knitted 'love-knots.'"—
Athenæum.
"A pleasant, healthy novel, full of life and spirit."—*Sunday Times.*

HER DESERTS. By Mrs. ALEXANDER FRASER.
Second Edition. 3 vols.

FIXED AS FATE. By Mrs. HOUSTOUN, Author of
"Recommended to Mercy," &c. 3 vols.

HURST & BLACKETT'S STANDARD LIBRARY

11. MARGARET AND HER BRIDESMAIDS.

"We recommend all who are in search of a fascinating novel to read this work for themselves. They will find it well worth their while. There are a freshness and originality about it quite charming."—*Athenæum.*

12. THE OLD JUDGE. By SAM SLICK.

"The publications included in this Library have all been of good quality; many give information while they entertain, and of that class the book before us is a specimen. The manner in which the Cheap Editions forming the series is produced, deserves especial mention. The paper and print are unexceptionable; there is a steel engraving in each volume, and the outsides of them will satisfy the purchaser who likes to see books in handsome uniform."—*Examiner.*

13. DARIEN. By ELIOT WARBURTON.

"This last production of the author of 'The Crescent and the Cross' has the same elements of a very wide popularity. It will please its thousands."—*Globe.*

14. FAMILY ROMANCE.

BY SIR BERNARD BURKE, ULSTER KING OF ARMS.

"It were impossible to praise too highly this most interesting book."—*Standard.*

15. THE LAIRD OF NORLAW. By MRS. OLIPHANT

"The 'Laird of Norlaw' fully sustains the author's high reputation."—*Sunday Times*

16. THE ENGLISHWOMAN IN ITALY.

"Mrs. Gretton's book is interesting, and full of opportune instruction."—*Times.*

17. NOTHING NEW.

BY THE AUTHOR OF "JOHN HALIFAX, GENTLEMAN."

"'Nothing New' displays all those superior merits which have made 'John Halifax' one of the most popular works of the day."—*Post.*

18. FREER'S LIFE OF JEANNE D'ALBRET.

"Nothing can be more interesting than Miss Freer's story of the life of Jeanne D'Albret, and the narrative is as trustworthy as it is attractive."—*Post.*

19. THE VALLEY OF A HUNDRED FIRES.

BY THE AUTHOR OF "MARGARET AND HER BRIDESMAIDS."

"If asked to classify this work, we should give it a place between 'John Halifax' and 'The Caxtons.'"—*Standard.*

20. THE ROMANCE OF THE FORUM.

BY PETER BURKE, SERGEANT AT LAW.

"A work of singular interest, which can never fail to charm."—*Illustrated News.*

21. ADELE. By JULIA KAVANAGH.

"'Adele' is the best work we have read by Miss Kavanagh; it is a charming story, full of delicate character-painting."—*Athenæum.*

22. STUDIES FROM LIFE.

BY THE AUTHOR OF "JOHN HALIFAX, GENTLEMAN."

"These 'Studies from Life' are remarkable for graphic power and observation. The book will not diminish the reputation of the accomplished author."—*Saturday Review.*

23. GRANDMOTHER'S MONEY.

"We commend 'Grandmother's Money' to readers in search of a good novel. The characters are true to human nature, and the story is interesting."—*Athenæum.*

24. A BOOK ABOUT DOCTORS. By J. C. JEAFFRESON.

"A delightful book."—*Athenæum.* "A book to be read and re-read; fit for the study as well as the drawing-room table and the circulating library."—*Lancet.*

14

HURST & BLACKETT'S STANDARD LIBRARY

15

39. THE WOMAN'S KINGDOM.

BY THE AUTHOR OF "JOHN HALIFAX, GENTLEMAN."

"'The Woman's Kingdom' sustains the author's reputation as a writer of the purest and noblest kind of domestic stories.—*Athenæum.*

40. ANNALS OF AN EVENTFUL LIFE.

BY GEORGE WEBBE DASENT, D.C.L.

"A racy, well-written, and original novel The interest never flags. The whole work sparkles with wit and humour."—*Quarterly Review.*

41. DAVID ELGINBROD. By GEORGE MAC DONALD.

"The work of a man of genius. It will attract the highest class of readers."—*Times.*

42. A BRAVE LADY. By the Author of "John Halifax."

"A very good novel; a thoughtful, well-written book, showing a tender, sympathy with human nature, and permeated by a pure and noble spirit."—*Examiner.*

43. HANNAH. By the Author of "John Halifax."

" A very pleasant, healthy story, well and artistically told. The book is sure of a wide circle of readers. The character of Hannah is one of rare beauty."—*Standard.*

44. SAM SLICK'S AMERICANS AT HOME.

"This is one of the most amusing books that we ever read."—*Standard.*

45. THE UNKIND WORD.

BY THE AUTHOR OF "JOHN HALIFAX, GENTLEMAN."

"The author of 'John Halifax' has written many fascinating stories, but we can call to mind nothing from her pen that has a more enduring charm than the graceful sketches in this work."—*United Service Magazine.*

46. A ROSE IN JUNE. By MRS. OLIPHANT.

"' A Rose in June ' is as pretty as its title. The story is one of the best and most touching which we owe to the industry and talent of Mrs. Oliphant, and may hold its own with even ' The Chronicles of Carlingford.' "—*Times.*

47. MY LITTLE LADY. By E. F. POYNTER.

"There is a great deal of fascination about this book. The author writes in a clear, unaffected style; she has a decided gift for depicting character, while the descriptions of scenery convey a distinct pictorial impression to the reader."—*Times.*

48. PHŒBE, JUNIOR. By MRS. OLIPHANT.

"This novel shows great knowledge of human nature. The interest goes on growing to the end. Phœbe is excellently drawn."—*Times.*

49. LIFE OF MARIE ANTOINETTE.

BY PROFESSOR CHARLES DUKE YONGE.

" A work of remarkable merit and interest, which will, we doubt not, become the most popular English history of Marie Antoinette."—*Spectator.*
"This book is well written, and of thrilling interest."—*Academy.*

50. SIR GIBBIE. By GEORGE MAC DONALD, LL.D.

"'Sir Gibbie' is a book of genius."—*Pall Mall Gazette.*
"This book has power, pathos, and humour. There is not a character which is not lifelike."—*Athenæum.*

51. YOUNG MRS. JARDINE.

BY THE AUTHOR OF "JOHN HALIFAX, GENTLEMAN."

"'Young Mrs. Jardine' is a pretty story, written in pure English."—*The Times.*
"There is much good feeling in this book. It is pleasant and wholesome."—*Athenæum.*

52. LORD BRACKENBURY. By AMELIA B. EDWARDS.

" A very readable story. The author has well conceived the purpose of high-class novel-writing, and succeeded in no small measure in attaining it. There is plenty of variety, cheerful dialogue, and general ' verve' in the book."—*Athenæum.*
"'Lord Brackenbury' is pleasant reading from beginning to end."—*Academy.*

www.ingramcontent.com/pod-product-compliance
Lightning Source LLC
Chambersburg PA
CBHW060608030726
47498CB00005B/1587